TRAPPED BY CLOCKS AND HEARTS

TRAPPED BY CLOCKS AND HEARTS

S. R. BREAKER

Zeta Indie Publishing

For Ally

Sweet dreams.

Contents

Dedication   V

Prologue   2

1   Chapter One - Rabb   8

2   Chapter Two - My Hero   15

3   Chapter Three - The Clock   23

4   Chapter Four - Pick Your Poison   29

5   Chapter Five - Allie's Lab   41

6   Chapter Six - The Bad Guy   54

7   Chapter Seven - Shadows   63

8   Chapter Eight - Caucus   76

9   Chapter Nine - Curious   85

10 Chapter Ten - Beware Rainbows   94

11 Chapter Eleven - Meet the Duchess   109

12 Chapter Twelve - Heartlamp   119

13 Chapter Thirteen - Curiouser   128

14 Chapter Fourteen - Fork in the Road ... 140

15 Chapter Fifteen - Ghosts ... 149

16 Chapter Sixteen - Just a Spell ... 161

17 Chapter Seventeen - And Curiouser ... 167

18 Chapter Eighteen - Queen of Hearts ... 180

19 Chapter Nineteen - I Chose This ... 193

20 Chapter Twenty - Eligible ... 199

21 Chapter Twenty-One - The Truth ... 213

22 Chapter Twenty-Two - Heartfire ... 219

23 Chapter Twenty-Three - Home ... 233

About The Author ... 239

Sneak Peek: Curse Of The Dragon Heir ... 241

Sneak Peek: The Selfless Series ... 246

In the Land of Wünder,
where certain myths are true,
there is treasure at the end of rainbows
and gears of ticking Clocks count on you.

The most potent of magics only contained
In the fervent beats of feelings' doors
Such mortal valves hold boundless power
And the Queen of Hearts wants yours.

Prologue

A gust of wind blew the heavy steel hatch open. Metal hinges creaking with age, the door slammed back against its frame built into the top-level dwelling of the ancient clock tower.

A forbidding structure standing tall in the middle of a vast desert, the tower's massive clock face momentarily lit up with a flash of lightning as the centuries-old spire almost succumbed to the onslaught of unnatural forces of magic that whipped against its façade.

Light rain pattered against the railing of the rigid balcony twisted around the dwelling, accompanying the crackle of thunder and more lightning.

With a flutter of a thick, hooded cloak and pale, blond hair, the shadowy figure that rode the ominous, rumbling clouds rolling in drifted closer.

The entire surroundings seemed to hush as he touched down on the balcony. Still in a fog-like cover of black smoke, it was difficult to make out his entire form, except that he appeared to be carrying something large in his arms as he walked through the door.

"You're late."

The hooded sorcerer glared at the tone of judgment from the disproportionately large head of the fuzzy cat that was lounging on the ratty couch in the cramped space of the dwelling. Despite being matted in places, the cat's fur swirled with different patterns of luminous whorls in shades of violet accompanying the animal's movements.

The sorcerer should have been bemused at the judgmental, critical tone of the cat, who should presume that *he* was late when they'd had no prior appointment whatsoever. Moreover, he didn't own the cat. Nor had he been expecting the cat to have been waiting for him.

But his mind was otherwise largely preoccupied.

His deep voice gruff, the sorcerer nudged the animal off the couch with the toe of his boot. "What are you doing here?"

The cat hissed as he jumped away, padded paws landing with soft thumps on the bare, wooden floor. "My fair mistress sent me to check on you, as usual."

Tail swishing to and fro, the cat pounced onto the back of the couch to watch as the sorcerer set the frigid body of the young woman he was carrying down onto it.

"Aren't you supposed to leave the bodies where they were?" the cat drawled. "The wretched Queen only needs their hearts."

Shrugging his hood down, damp hair in his eyes, the sorcerer bent beside the couch with a frown to assess the girl's condition.

Ice covered her from the top of her long brown hair to the toes of her tasseled shoes. Unconscious, eyes closed, her face a pale blue, she appeared ghost-like, as though petrified, even perhaps already dead. Her stiff white lab coat overlay an off-white frilled shirt and suspenders over moleskin pants. Edges heavy with water, her hair and clothes were beginning to take on a glossy quality as the ice melt dripped on the floor.

The cat tilted his head. "You're already the best assassin in the land. Do you still need to be such an overachiever?"

The sorcerer narrowed his stormy blue eyes. "Don't make me kill you, cat. If memory serves, you are down to significantly fewer than nine lives." With a rustle of his cloak, he drew out a container, a glass sphere framed with an ornate, polished brass metal cage adorned with intricate filigree patterns.

What sat within the sphere was a bean-shaped lump—about the size of a fist.

Such an object should have looked ordinary.

Except that it flickered with a deep, fiery orange glow, casting a dim light across the room as the object throbbed within the almost opaque glass.

"Oh, good, you've got the Heartlamp," the cat had begun to remark. "The Queen's envoy is on their way to investigate your delay—" The sorcerer slipped his hand into his pocket again and retrieved yet another bean-shaped lump.

Except this one was different.

The cat stopped short, eyes widening. "Whoa, what the hell are you doing with one of those outside a Heartlamp? And in your pocket no less!"

"This one is hers." He gestured to the motionless form on the couch.

Unlike the first lump, this one wasn't glowing dim like an ember, nor emitting a subtle halo of wispy smoke. It didn't throb as though alive. It merely sat like a rock in the middle of his palm.

Eyeing the rock, the cat scoffed. "What's wrong with her heart? You can't bring it to the Queen like that."

"It's not empty."

"It looks empty," the cat pointed out. "It's useless."

Pressing his lips together, the sorcerer stared at the heart in his hand. "I sensed a veiled power," he relayed. "And when I took it out, I..." He stopped short and met the cat's curious gaze, as if then deciding that now was not the proper time to get into it. "That's why I took longer. I needed to find another girl to fetch another heart." He gestured to the occupied Heartlamp. "The Queen still needs one."

Curling into a lounging position on the edge of the couch, the cat licked a paw. "What are you going to do with that one then? Put it back inside her?"

The sorcerer shook his head. "It's too risky." Another commotion as of rolling thunder stole his attention and his gaze snapped up toward the sky.

The cat seemed unperturbed. "The Queen's envoy nears. Maybe you can present the Queen that strange heart anyway."

The sorcerer's forehead creased in clear hesitation. He set the already occupied glass vessel on a table and stared at it in deep thought.

The cat noticed his gaze. "My mistress doesn't have any more Heartlamps lying about in case you're wondering. She sends only one, per the Queen's request," the cat relayed. "And even if you ask, she will need time to craft you another one—by which time that extracted heart will have long withered away."

The furrow in the sorcerer's eyebrows deepened. "Shut up and let me think, cat."

The commotion outside the clock tower increased in intensity.

"Whatever." The cat flopped to one side. "If anyone finds you with that rogue heart, guess whose head is coming off? The Queen grants you more freedom than most because of the nature of your existence and your duties, but surely a transgression such as this will not work in your favor." The cat's eyes lit up in a memory as it went on, "Remember what happened with the Knave of Hearts? Hoo boy! And he only stole those tarts, not totems of mystical power."

"I said shut up, cat," the sorcerer snapped. He squared his shoulders as he straightened up and took a deep breath as if to get ready. Then clutching the unbeating heart in his hand, the sorcerer raised his hand to his chest.

The cat's yellow eyes widened as he watched.

Wincing, the sorcerer pressed his fingers through his clothes and against the resistance of his flesh. His hollow chest emitted a pale blue glow until his fingers were plunged deep inside—his form glowed brighter, just before chains of light streaked through the air and a rising gale whipped through the room.

Crackling electricity filled the dwelling within the clock tower, its brightness nearly blinding as it surged outward, and a pulsing wave of energy shunted through everything all at once. The sheer force of the magic threw the cat tumbling behind the couch with a screech.

For a moment, a pale blue shimmer covered the sorcerer's entire figure.

Not hurt at all, the cat sprang up to peer over the back of the couch again. His eyes were wide as the glow around the sorcerer's body began to dissipate.

"Whoa," the cat remarked. "How does it feel to have a fresh heart in there after being empty all this time?"

Almost panting, the sorcerer straightened up again. His forehead still creased, he swallowed hard but did not respond.

The cat tilted his head again, the expression on his face a mix of amusement and awe as it breathed, "I can't believe you just did that."

The sorcerer shot the cat a glare that could cut but did not respond. With an easy wave of his hand, a cloak of shadow covered the form on the couch entirely before the girl disappeared from view, camouflaged. He turned to give the cat a meaningful look. "You will tell no one about this." And with another flutter of his cloak, he spun around to head to the door to meet with the Queen's envoy.

The cat mewled after him. "Hey, what about the girl?"

The sorcerer paused in mid-stride but for a moment. "I suppose we'll have to wait for her to thaw out. And once I have my answers, I can kill her."

***

I

Chapter One - Rabb

I couldn't breathe.

Almost imperceptibly slower today, the dull ticking of the giant clock echoed hollow around me. Creaks and groans filled the old tower's structure, the gentle, rhythmic ticking and clinking of massive metal gears and mechanical workings, amidst the occasional howling winds of the remote corner of the land I called home.

Desolate.

Quiet.

It had been so for centuries.

And I liked it that way.

I grasped at the collar of my shirt in an attempt to catch my breath, to escape from this unknown stifling sensation.

I glanced up from my wooden desk to look around.

My loft was nestled within the top of the clock tower, its worn furnishings and faded velvet drapes from the tall windows blending seamlessly with the clock's inner workings. Small. Functional. But the place was never so unkempt as it was today.

Piles of books were haphazardly strewn, scrolls and papers cluttered about the floor. Dusty shelves previously only used to store bottles of ale had become host to a disarray of mismatched paraphernalia as I had spent the better part of the last three weeks head buried in my research.

I'd barely slept, barely eaten.

Yet still, what I was searching for eluded me.

I should have been content with my life. I was the most powerful sorcerer assassin for hire in the land. I could have anything I wanted. There was absolutely nothing I could want for.

Except perhaps answers...

For questions that hadn't plagued me at all until quite recently.

The perpetual cloud cover of my desert home permitted scant streaks of sunlight to filter through the skies. According to the reliable clock, that was built and has been running without requiring fine-tuning for centuries, it was mid-morning.

Sitting back in my seat, I frowned as I took a deep breath. My nose was stuffed, my throat constricting for no apparent reason. I slammed my fist on the table, rattling the bottle of brandy sufficiently enough for my snifter to tip over and its contents to spill over my papers.

Oh, for god's sake.

Burying my face into my hand, I groaned at the telltale alarm.

Ignoring the splattered mess, I stood abruptly, my chair scraping the wooden floor as it pushed back. "What the hell is she doing?"

Stopping to take a deep breath, I closed my eyes to locate that girl in my mind. I stopped short, my frown deepening, and with a loud, grumbling sigh, I whirled to grab my cloak off the hook by the door and teleported away.

With a burst of smoke, I reappeared above a lush, green landscape.

My nose twitched at the pungent scent of earth from the recent rain mingling with the fragrant trees wafting up to me. The cheery, yellow sun was bright in the sky amongst an assortment of fluffy, white clouds. The air was alive with the cawing, hoots, and howls of the forest animals.

Nothing at all like my remote, desolate corner of the world.

Tulgey Woods was a deceptive place. From a distance, it appeared to be a serene and peaceful forest, filled with charming little animals, and trees and flowers that were wont to chat you up if you dallied for too long.

But the wood was actually the home of a monstrous creature.

With eyes of flame, jaws that bite, and claws that catch, it would arrive like a dark shadow to engulf the entire forest if it sensed even a smidge of mystical power on its grounds.

Not exactly an ideal place to go gallivanting.

Spotting the young woman emerge from the darkness of the forest, my breathing eased a little. She probably almost got suffocated by the trees and flowers in the thick woods, but had fortunately made it out before any of the more carnivorous plants caught her scent.

Folding my arms across my chest, I hovered atop a Tum-tum tree a few yards away.

Walking up toward a giant mushroom in a clearing, the girl tucked back her unruly brown hair blowing in the slight breeze. Her long, white lab coat fluttered behind her like a cape. She still wore the same clothes she was wearing when I'd found her.

The mystical fungus a shade too tall for her to prop her elbows on, the girl leaned on the tiptoes of her loafers to regard an inordinately large caterpillar that was perched upon it with a narrow-eyed look. "Hello?"

Not startled at all at the sight of her, the languid blue creature, three feet tall with a slimy, semi-transparent body, puffed smoke out from his gaudy hookah. "Who are *you*?"

The girl's nose wrinkled in deep thought. "You know...I actually really *literally* don't know."

The pipe of the hookah poised near its mouth, the caterpillar shot her a look of ridicule. "What do you mean by that? Explain yourself!"

She chewed on her inner cheek, her tone matter-of-fact. "Oh, I don't really understand it all myself so I'm afraid I can't tell you who I really am. See?"

The caterpillar folded its arms across its chest. "I don't see."

"It's just...I can't seem to remember things."

"Can't remember *what* things?" the caterpillar prompted.

She frowned in contemplation. "Well, I heard I was found in an icy cave in the frozen wastes, left for dead. One of your world's wizard guys rescued me. But when I woke up, I didn't remember anything. Who I was." She twirled a lock of hair around her index finger. "How I got here. Where I'm from."

Wizard? My eyebrows snapped together in distaste at the term.

And how did she know what had happened anyway?

She wasn't even telling it right—since I absolutely *did not* rescue her.

I wasn't supposed to be at the frozen wasteland that day, those remote fringes along Wünder which people rarely visited, since I was in the middle of an assignment from the Queen.

But when I investigated inside that small, almost hidden cave, I'd found her.

Alone. Frozen. Nearly dead.

Then again, it wasn't unusual.

Unscrupulous, or perhaps desperate, citizens often froze to death attempting to brave the many frigid frozen wastelands in search of mystical Heartfire embers.

The Queen certainly wasn't handing them out. No, the Queen hired sorcerers like me to seek out and extract Heartfire magic from arguably its easiest source.

Thus, after a quick assessment determined that the girl was still alive, naturally, my first instinct had been to harvest her heart.

It should have been simple.

I would have left her body, delivered her heart to the Queen, and gone back to my clock tower to enjoy my life of solitude until I was called to duty once again.

End of story.

It wasn't.

For the last couple of weeks, the strange young woman had spent delirious days in bed, indisposed, recovering from frostbite and near death. Installed in the little storage studio beneath my loft, I had successfully hidden her presence from the Queen's envoys and the rest of the world—for now.

I had even intentionally selected to bed women who, while additionally skilled in medical training to check in on her to ensure her survival, were also steadfast with discretion. No mean feat.

So far, all I'd managed to gather by the reports from my women were hints that, judging by the girl's clothing and manner of speaking, she may not be from Wünder altogether, which was a mystery in itself. Not to mention the fact that, for some reason, apparently, magic amazed her. It seemed that, to her, everything here was bizarre and new.

Since she wasn't yet fit for questioning, I hadn't spoken more than five words to her, let alone had any opportunities to tell her anything about what had happened. She couldn't possibly have known about the cave.

Of course, there was no accounting for her guile. I didn't know her at all. For starters, I couldn't fathom how she'd escaped my tower to get all the way to this forest. According to the last report I had received, the girl was still meant to be bedridden, supposedly too weak.

She must have recovered faster than she was letting on. She *must* have been sneaking around and eavesdropping the other day when that cat had dropped by again to snoop around and prattle my ear off about things.

A nerve ticked in my cheek in my annoyance. *I swear to god—*

I was going to gut that cat the next time I saw it.

After I gutted *her*.

"Who are you?" the caterpillar snapped again.

The girl winced at the creature's brusque response but she probably figured she might as well respond. "I guess you can call me Allie," she declared, looking a bit miffed. "Honestly, it's been quite a rough few weeks. I mean, if you forgot who you were, and found yourself in a strange place, you could probably really use something to relax too, couldn't you?"

"Not a bit."

Allie's forehead creased. "Why am I even having this discussion with a talking caterpillar?" Shaking her head, she blinked a few times before turning away.

"Come back!" the caterpillar called out. "I've something important to say!"

She glanced over her shoulder. "What is it?"

"You'll get used to it in no time," the caterpillar stated, put the hookah back into its mouth, and began smoking again.

She looked around, at a loss. "What, you mean being here?"

The caterpillar took the hookah out of its mouth once more and yawned. Then it began to slither slowly down off the mushroom, crawling away on the grass, merely remarking as it went, "One side will bring you up, and the other side will bring you down."

Her lips pursed. "The sides of *what*?"

"Of the mushroom," the caterpillar finished before it disappeared into the woods.

Just then, a low rumbling from across the valley caught my attention. Glancing up, I clenched my jaw.

Here it comes.

The shadow.

2

Chapter Two - My Hero

A large flock of birds squawked and flapped upward from a clump of trees on the horizon, a flurry in their efforts to escape the eclipse that blotted out the light like a tidal wave of darkness visibly coming closer and closer to the clearing where the giant mushroom stood.

Letting out a haggard sigh, I rode the air to coast swiftly down, scooping the girl up in my arms before she even noticed I had arrived.

"Whoa—" She grabbed my neck to secure herself against me before she looked up to meet my gaze. "It's you!"

I was sure she could read the disapproval in my eyes, the wind whipping past us as I flew us away from the forest.

But her cheeks were pink, her smile wide with pleasure.

It was odd. Since I had found her, I'd left her to herself, presuming she required more rest, presuming my companions were more than capable of dealing with her.

Perhaps I should have cared about who she was, why she had been in that cave, where she was from. But my only interest was to solve the puzzle of this mysterious heart.

I had only seen her once while she recovered from her state.

That time I'd had to physically come downstairs to deliver her food. Still bedridden, the expression in her tired eyes when they met mine was most definitely not delight. Apprehension, yes, but not delight.

Definitely not pleasure.

This situation did not warrant the pleasure in her eyes.

Then it hit me.

That damn caterpillar.

"What did you just eat?" I asked in suspicion.

Her pupils dilated, she laughed merrily. "Oh, don't be such a downer." She'd clearly sampled some of that caterpillar's mushroom when I wasn't looking.

I shook my head again. "Don't you know what magic mushrooms do?"

"It didn't look poisonous. It didn't say poison on it." Her face fixed into mock sobriety. "Besides, you know what they say. If at first, you don't succeed, try two more times so that your failure is statistically significant."

I scoffed in ridicule. "You are so intoxicated right now."

She smacked her lips out loud. "It tasted like waffles. Did you know everything in this world tastes like waffles to me? Besides, the caterpillar made it sound so fascinating. I was just curious."

"You are much too curious for your own good," I mumbled.

"I'm a scientist." She threw up one hand as if to gesture the obvious.

I narrowed my eyes at her. "How is it that you remember you are a scientist when you don't remember anything else about yourself?" Even with my arms hooked under her back and legs, I motioned air quotes with my fingers. "*Allie.*"

Laughing again, she pinched my cheek. "Are you always this surly?"

Flinching in horrified protest, I recoiled away. "Stop that!"

Allie was much too delirious. She looked around, seemingly only then noticing where we were. "Oh, we're flying! Look, I'm a bird! I can see above the trees!" She threw her head back. "How am I so high up? Where are my feet?"

Fuming in my chest, I gritted my teeth.

My god, she was so annoying.

I was severely tempted to shove her away and toss her against the rocky mountain peaks beneath us to her certain death.

I imagined the feeling of satisfaction at watching her fall, the symphony of her cracking bones, the vivid red gushing of blood from her eyes, her mouth... Not that I enjoyed death. I was rarely capable of enjoying things to begin with. But it would likely be a relief to be discharged of this responsibility.

If only her entire existence wasn't potentially the answer to my biggest problem.

Out of the corner of my eye, the dark shadow behind us was beginning to engulf Tulgey Woods. Howling animals and stampeding creatures tried to outrun the monstrous wave of sludge that was undulating from beneath the ground as the Jabberwocky's massive head prepared to emerge to gobble everything up.

In Allie's hypersensitive state, it was difficult to know

what would set her off, especially if faced with such a horrifying view, so I clasped her head against my chest so she wouldn't see.

Keeping my grip around her, I waved my fingers to cast a spell, blanketing the entire forest with fog before coasting faster on the wind. In the distance, where the forest greens gradually faded into the stark brown of my desert, I could finally sight the top of my clock tower.

Allie's voice was muffled in my chest. "Wow, you're like really protective considering we've only just met. Are you in love with me or something?"

Glancing down to meet her gaze in ridicule, I groaned inwardly. "Please tell me you took a piece from the other side of the mushroom too."

"Of course I did."

"Eat it then," I ordered.

She mocked-mouthed the same words back before popping the morsel in her mouth.

Before long, I was touching down on the balcony outside the top of my clock tower.

I set her on her feet and pulled my arms away, but she was still clinging around my neck. I pursed my lips. "You can let go now."

Allie's face was tilted up toward mine. She was no longer laughing but her cheeks were still flushed. Her body was pressed against mine, and despite the cold wind, her warmth wrapped around me.

I had to blink a few times to keep my wits. My head was getting a tad bit fuzzy as well. Meeting her gaze steadily, I glared down at her. "What?"

She swooned up at me. "My hero."

Ugh. That was the last thing I was.

Allie regarded me with an appraising look. "I just realized I never caught your name. Do you have one?"

My response was more of a grunt than a word. "Rabb."

Her honey-colored eyes glazed over as she searched my face, her voice hushed as she proposed, "You know...it's okay if you want to kiss me, Rabb. I mean, I'm pretty sure I've been kissed before, so you can if you want."

I couldn't help another roll of my eyes.

With her wavy hair fluttering in the breeze, marble-smooth skin, elegant nose, and full lips, I would imagine normal men would have considered her pretty, even beautiful. Her clothing lacked style, which didn't flatter her figure at all, but her soft, inviting curves indeed rivaled those of my regular companions.

But I had no time for tenderness like kissing or, indeed, love. I did require companionship now and again but I'd never felt anything for those women.

A heartless assassin for the Queen would only be so effective if he had been indeed rendered incapable of feelings.

And being the most notorious assassin serving the Queen of Hearts, who ruled over the land, my sole purpose was to seduce the women of Wünder to complacence in order to steal their hearts to deliver to the Queen for her consumption.

My kisses were weapons. And rarely did I even need to go that far. In the past, kingdoms had fallen from a mere smile from me. Maidens, queens, princesses, and the occasional prince now and again threw themselves at my feet to entreat a kind word from my lips—right before I tore their hearts out.

One look from me would make any female within a ten-mile radius melt where she stood.

Usually.

Not moving an inch otherwise, I glared at Allie some more. "Great, good to know. Now sober the hell up."

She tilted her head to one side. "I watched you seduce that girl who came by the other day. You were really good at that."

I groaned again. So she *had* been spying on me for the last few weeks.

But I didn't respond. With another even glare, I watched her face for a few moments, waiting as the effects of the intoxicating magic mushroom visibly lifted from her features.

When Allie seemed to get her bearings back, her mouth dropped open a slight. She pulled her arms away from me to straighten herself up.

She shook her head, blinking several times. "Oh. Well." Clearing her throat, she dusted off her clothes. "That was highly inconvenient."

"You think?" I huffed and whirled around to stomp through the metal door. "So you're feeling better, I take it? How did you even get to Tulgey Woods?"

"Well...it was rather odd. Quite inexplicably, I found a door in a tree when I was..." She paused. "Exploring. I'd never seen a door in a tree before so I was curious. I know it doesn't make any sense but it's true."

I merely rolled my eyes again. I didn't understand why she had deemed it inexplicable. In fact, I should have known. Many trees in Wünder concealed hollows which led to other places. Certain animals used them for migration and hunting food.

Following at my heels, she cleared her throat again and put her hand out. "We haven't officially met."

"We don't need to officially meet."

"So...you're some kind of wizard?"

"I'm a sorcerer," I corrected, miffed.

She wrinkled her nose. "Like there's a difference."

"Don't make me kill you after I just saved your life." I shot her a dark look. "*Do not* try to escape again."

She shifted on her feet. "I wasn't trying to escape. I just...wanted to take a look around. Aren't you really overreacting about this whole thing?" She put her hands up in a shrug to drawl, "Besides, I wasn't in '*danger*' danger."

I gritted my teeth again. I seriously wanted to wring her insolent neck. "And yet, I still had to save you. Next time, maybe I should just let the Jabberwocky get you." I stopped at the top of the staircase leading down to the studio and gestured my arm pointedly for her to descend.

Her forehead creased in confusion once more. "The...what? Ugh, never mind." Her expression morphed into aggravated, molten disdain and she folded her arms across her chest. "You know what, yes. Of course, I was trying to escape! I've been locked up in this tower for weeks. I understand I've been sick, and I appreciate your efforts in restoring me to health, but you honestly can't keep me locked up in here forever."

Impatient with her stalling, I turned to head back to my desk, my response offhand, authoritative but steady. "It's for your own safety. Your life is as precious to me as my own."

Her tone still soured. "What the hell does that even mean?"

"It means—" I whirled around to face her. "You are not to endanger yourself again."

Eyes wide, the indignation was raw on her face. "I don't even know where I am! I don't even know *who* I am or what the hell I'm doing—"

"What you are is *mine*," I pressed. "Now stay downstairs. Stay out of trouble. Be quiet. And don't make the notion of killing you even more tempting than it already is."

"None of this makes any sense!" She threw her hands up.

My reply dripped with sarcasm and finality. "Welcome to Wünder."

She winced as though I'd struck her but she didn't say anything more. She spun around to storm off, stomping all the way down the staircase.

3

Chapter Three - The Clock

The metal hatch behind me slammed shut as if by itself.

I shot the door a narrow-eyed look before spotting the purple-striped cat meander across the floor.

His blue swirly gaze met mine. "My, my, what's going on here? Trouble in paradise?"

He was clearly amused.

I strolled toward my desk. "What the hell are you doing here again, cat?"

"My mistress sends me again as usual." Padded feet barely making a sound, the cat hopped up onto my table, right by my spilled snifter of brandy that had soaked through things.

I peeled up the wet scrolls before instantly dropping them in distaste. "Does the Duchess have nothing better to do than to snoop on my personal affairs?"

"You know she will keep sending me until you give her what she wants."

"That's out of the question." I slumped back into my seat, rubbing my temples.

"So you say."

I shot the cat another dagger look and he merely chuckled, dropping the subject.

"Did your little pet escape the tower?"

"Don't even start with me, Chez."

"Rabb, it's been three weeks," the cat pointed out. "Don't you think your 'let's wait until she gets her memory back' plan needs a little adjusting by now? I told you, you should have turned her over to the Queen from the get-go."

I checked the time on my pocket watch. "The other day *you* said she was growing on you," I reminded him as I was fully aware that the cat had frequently been downstairs to visit with the girl. Just curious, Chez had said.

"What can I say, she gives good belly rubs. Still, I don't want my head cut off when the Queen finds out." Chez gave me his trademark grin. "Who else is going to put up with your surly ass—who has *already* put up with your surly ass for the better part of a hundred years, hey, Rabb? I mean, I'm practically your best friend." He paused to consider. "Heck, I'm your only friend."

I shot the cat a glare.

I didn't need friends. I didn't need anyone.

I frowned. My chest felt tight just then, and to my absolute consternation, hot tears began to well up in my eyes.

I blinked back the wretched stinging. "Oh dammit, she's crying." Reaching over to the nearest pipe, I pounded my fist on it several times, the dull banging echoing throughout the clock tower structure. "Oi, down there!" I yelled out. "Stop crying!"

Chez's eyes were as wide as two yellow moons. "How could you possibly know that? What is going on? Are you feeling what *she's* feeling?" He stopped, jaw dropping. "More to the point, are you actually *feeling*?"

I lowered my head. I supposed my secret was bound to come out sooner or later. In fact, it was a wonder that Chez hadn't already caught on to it earlier, given he was *always* here. I let out a sigh. "I think so. Because I carry her heart." I shook my head briskly. "This has never happened before."

"I knew you'd been getting more testy lately," the cat mused. "How long has this been going on?"

"Three weeks."

Chez's jaw dropped again. "And you didn't tell me?"

I dismissed him with a wave. "It seems one-sided. I thought it would go away," I relayed. "I thought it could have been a temporary side effect from taking in her heart. It *might* still be a temporary side effect. Why do you think I'm working so hard to figure out how to get rid of it?" I gestured my arm across the piles of books and papers all over the room.

Chez licked a paw. "Hearts can't exist outside a body for too long."

Already knowing that, I nodded. "I'll need a new Heart-lamp."

"Without the Queen's command, that will be tricky," Chez relayed.

"Still, I need to do something. Since you already know

what's going on, why can't you ask the Duchess for me?" I pressed.

Chez gave me a pointed look. "You know she'll say no if I ask. She'll want *you* to ask."

"I figured as much." I rubbed the bridge of my nose with my fingers. "I need to make sure that girl stays out of trouble in the meanwhile."

"Good luck with that. She seems to be a feisty one." Chez grinned. "Remind me again why you can't just kill her?"

I tried not to pause too long before responding. "I need her alive."

Chez blew out a breath. "I think you have finally gone mad, my friend," he remarked. "I don't even know what in Wünder possessed you to take in that dubious empty heart—like—like you had nothing left to lose..." The cat trailed off, tilting its head. "Wait a minute. Is it...happening?"

Pursing my lips, I looked out the window. This clock tower was not only my home. My existence was bound to it, and each ticking of the clock was a guarantee of my continued survival. But lately...

"The clock has...been slowing of late. I've noticed."

Chez frowned in concern. "Your life clock? The countdown has begun? Isn't it a few centuries too early? Has time gone by so fast?"

I shook my head. "I'm not sure what's going on. I was assured the clock shouldn't slow for at least another six decades." I stood up in a huff. "This is why I needed her heart. I had no choice."

Chez nodded. "I wondered why you were so reckless, taking in that strange heart."

I fiddled with the ink pot on my desk. "That cave where I found her... I detected a faint mystical energy, the nature of which I hadn't encountered in a long, long time. And when I extricated her heart from her chest, there was a brief spark of power, and despite its inert appearance, I could tell it contains significantly powerful magic."

I gave Chez a meaningful look. "This girl... I think her heart is a *coeur*."

The cat's eyes widened again. "It's a what? No way! Those were just old wives' tales. Are you talking about the legendary Heartfire ember of perpetual energy? I've never seen one before."

I dropped my gaze. "It could be a *coeur*."

Chez couldn't resist a quip, "Or it's just a useless lump of rock."

I clicked my tongue. "Perhaps it was not the best decision I've ever made in my life but if I'm right, I can't risk losing all that power. Especially now. My powers are deteriorating. I need hers. I only need to know how to unlock it."

"And the Queen?" Chez prompted.

"The Queen will definitely want her heart." I couldn't keep the gravity out of my tone. "She will know for sure it's not empty. She will know it's special. We're just lucky the Queen can't sense its power yet. But when that time comes, the Queen will definitely take it, and whatever chance I have of obtaining that power will be gone."

Chez stretched out on the desk. "Perhaps this is a too-obvious question but...have you tried asking the girl? Just seduce her. Make her fall in love with you already. She might be able to give you all the answers you seek."

I groaned again. "Don't you think I've thought of that? It's not that easy."

Chez's head quirked. "You've never had any problems before."

Frustrated, I waved his doubt away. "Well, this girl is…weird. For starters, she would rather stay downstairs than even so much as look at me. She talks of other worlds. Her heart is odd enough." Almost in derisive exasperation, I paused. "But I suppose I could try one last time."

"Either way," Chez rationalized, "if anyone detects that you're carrying around a rogue heart or hiding a captive girl who may or may not be from around here, there will be hell to pay."

I waved him away again. "I just need to think of another way to figure it all out."

Surely, I would be able to figure it all out.

My task was clear.

I needed to extract the mystical power from the *coeur*. And then once I stopped the countdown, I could dispose of the girl.

I wouldn't stop until I ensured my survival.

No matter the cost.

4

Chapter Four - Pick Your Poison

Leaning against the windowsill, I clanged on the metal pipe with the hilt of my pocket dagger. With the brass pipework wound all throughout the innards of the building, the banging echoed like a bell, ringing throughout the entire structure of the clock tower. There was no way she could have missed hearing it.

Even as hurried footsteps shuffling from beneath the floor indicated that Allie was coming up, I didn't stop. Even as I noted the top of her head gradually emerging from the winding staircase, I didn't stop.

When her eyes met mine, they were already wide with mock incredulity and expectation, and as if an unspoken act of protest, her walking slowed. The damn girl took her sweet, bloody time coming up, finally stopping to stand at the top of the staircase.

I stopped clanging on the pipe, sheathing the dagger back in its hilt at my hip.

Allie paused for another beat. Stuffing her hands in her lab coat pockets, her eyes dull, her tone as deadpan as ever, she finally spoke, "Oh. My. God. What?"

Resisting the urge to roll my eyes again, I gave the table by the window a careless wave.

"Supper."

Allie's eyes slid over and ever so slightly widened upon noticing the little round table draped in a rich, deep velvet cloth. A copper contraption sitting upon it emitted a soft whirring to keep the tea kettle steaming hot. Edison-bulb candles on golden candlesticks matched the polished brass cutlery and delicate clockwork-themed China. A pyramid of profiteroles and caramel-glazed cream puffs was surrounded by a delectable selection of cured meats, cheeses, dried and fresh fruit, and flowers. Long-stemmed crystal glasses gleamed underneath the glowing ball of witchlight hovering above the table, lending the corner a bit of cozy elegance.

She blinked a few times, half in astonishment, half still in suspicion. "What's all this?" Her eyebrow quirked up. "Is this...you apologizing to me?"

I retched in my head. "Don't be ridiculous. I just thought it might be...beneficial for us to..." I chose my words carefully, "share this meal tonight."

Down by my hip where Allie couldn't possibly see or notice, I curled my fingers ever so subtly, and the air thickened with the faintest yellow haze.

My spell was giving off enough pheromones to seduce any living being across my entire desert. A mole rat five miles away would have been tickled pink.

Allie tilted her head ever so slightly to regard me with a look.

Clenching my jaw, I watched for the telltale signs of her succumbing to my spell.

Her eyes didn't dilate. She didn't throw herself at my feet. She didn't move closer. She didn't do anything.

Those big hazel eyes merely narrowed. "What are you looking at me like that for?"

Perfectly frustrated, I released the breath I'd been holding.

Dammit. That was usually all it took. One look. One smile.

A corner of her mouth turned down in displeasure. "Look, I can take my meals downstairs on my little tray like the unwilling prisoner I clearly am." Allie whirled around to head back downstairs.

I called out, "Wait."

She paused in mid-turn, her eyes expectant. "What?"

I dropped my gaze. I was going to have to try a different tack.

Adopting a hesitant, diffident manner, I started again. "Hey. Look. You're right." I ran one hand through my hair. "The reason I asked you to dinner was to apologize to you. I am...sorry about what I said," I conceded, whilst crossing my fingers in my head.

Allie seemed to consider my words for a moment. "Well, I appreciate that." She cast the food another glance. "I suppose this does look lovely and you did go through all that trouble..."

I didn't comment. It only took a snap of my fingers but she could think whatever she wanted.

I sat down and gestured my arm for her to take the other seat.

Allie crossed the floor and sat down. Her eyes roved over the food, widening slightly again at the chocolate-covered pastries in particular. "I...this is all so..." Her eyes glowed when she looked up at me again. "This looks wonderful."

I'll bet. I sniffed inwardly.

The evening's spread was certainly a far cry from her daily rations of food that I'd been sending down.

I rarely ate this well myself. I certainly didn't need it fancy.

Leaning forward, I held her gaze solemnly. "I'm glad you like it," I said, using the deepest, most sultry voice I could muster through my annoyance.

Allie's smile remained reasonably pleasant. Her demeanor didn't change whatsoever.

For god's sake, wasn't I having any effect on her at all?

I had the sudden urge to flip the table over.

Instead, I clenched my jaw and reached for the liquor.

"Oh, here, let me." She jumped to offer, reaching over to pour two goblets of wine. Shifting in the padded, wrought-iron chair, she pursed her lips, remorse lacing her features. "I suppose I haven't really thanked you yet for rescuing me from the frozen wasteland, saving me from an icy death."

"I didn't rescue you," I corrected.

She flinched a little at my abruptness. "Alright. Then again I suppose you didn't strike me as the type."

Huffing, I reached for my wine to take a sip.

"I think I've hardly even seen you leave this tower in the

last three weeks," she mused, almost to herself. "Lounging about and drinking at your desk or cavorting with what I'm assuming is the local color. I guess you like to lead a dull, quiet, bachelor's life."

I turned a steely-eyed glare her way. She had no idea what the hell she was talking about. "For your information, I am the Queen of Hearts's most notorious assassin."

Her eyebrows rose, the look she gave me in response was nothing short of mocking. As if she was trying not to laugh.

I couldn't help narrowing my eyes. "I'm not making a joke. I am the most powerful sorcerer in Wünder."

She took a nonchalant bite of her food. "Sure."

I checked my urge to seethe in frustration. It didn't really matter what she believed. Why was I letting myself be bothered by it so much?

I took another big gulp of my wine.

Allie peered at the flaky pastry in her hand as if it piqued her interest more than I did.

Dammit.

The spell still wasn't working.

I had to up the ante a bit more.

"Would you like some more wine?" I grabbed her half-filled goblet in a hurried manner, and sure enough, I spilled some on my white shirt. "Oh."

Glancing up at me, Allie blinked in surprise, the spoonful of custard halfway up to her mouth.

"Sorry." Feigning displeasure, I stood up and began to unbutton my shirt.

Catching sight of myself in the reflection of the glassed-in exposed clockwork mechanism that made up the wall panel across the way, I almost smirked in triumph.

As to be expected, the nature of my work kept me in shape. The toned, taut muscles on my arms rippled as I shrugged off my shirt altogether. The dim lighting in my loft cast shadows across the contours of my well-defined chest and abdomen. One of my regular companions often gushed over what she called my 'sculpted physique'. I had a few scars here and there but certainly, the ladies had had no complaints.

Allie loaded a forkful of salad greens like absolutely nothing out of the ordinary was going on.

Was she totally blind?

Oh, for the love of—

Glaring at her, I sat back down, still shirtless.

I couldn't believe this was even happening.

This girl should be so incredibly, uncomfortably aroused by now. She should be wrapped around my pinky finger and begging to do me favors, begging to climb me.

With another brief look up at me and her mouth full of food, Allie mumbled, "Aren't you going to put another shirt on?"

My entire face suffused with heat. Though I wasn't sure if it was from embarrassment or insult. This was absolutely unprecedented.

Outside, a cacophony of faint howling echoed across the landscape of my desert. Every other living creature in the vicinity was no doubt having a time of it, having been triggered in serious heat from my spell.

Allie pushed a piece of tomato off to the side of her plate

and began to pick out more of the mushy fruit from her meal as though it was a wretched thing.

Suddenly feeling drained, I swallowed hard.

For some reason, I couldn't catch my breath. My throat was itchy. My skin clammy and hot. What in the actual hell was going on?

My head spun. I almost lost my balance, tipping to one side in my seat.

Allie watched me with wary, wide eyes. "Whoa. What's going on with you, big guy?"

Something was definitely, seriously wrong... But I couldn't quite pin it down. What was it?

Was I more fatigued than I realized from the lack of sleep and the strain of the rescue earlier today? Perhaps traveling all the way back from Tulgey Woods without teleporting expended a lot of my magic.

I felt weak. Feverish.

Allie tilted her head to regard me with a look. "Oh, hey, are you sick?"

I dropped my gaze in concern.

Could it be that because of the looming countdown, my mystical core was draining easier and I had become more susceptible to mortal nuisances such as being sick?

I rebelled at the thought. "I have never been sick before in my entire life."

She pursed her lips. "Maybe you caught a cold. I told you to put a shirt on. It's freezing in here," she noted with a gesture around us.

I stood again but I couldn't stay standing upright. I had

an incredible undeniable urge to shut my eyes. I swayed on my feet.

"Oh, shoot." Allie stood to catch me before I toppled over. With a roll of her eyes, she groaned in seeming resignation. "Fine, jeez, come on. Let's get you to bed. Looks like you need to have a little nap."

"I do not need a 'little nap'. I am—," I halted, almost slurring, "the most powerful sorcerer in Wünder."

Her tone was wan. "Yes, of course. Sure, you are. Now, give me your arm so I can help you walk."

I frowned. She was so exasperating. I wanted to muffle that smart mouth, possibly with a pillow. But no, I wouldn't just kill her. I would disassemble her piece by piece, feed her to the desert wolves, burn the leftover scraps...

"Ugh. God! How heavy are you?" Whining, she slung my arm around her shoulders.

Her bare neck was cool against my hot skin and I hissed under my breath.

"Whoa, hey, you're—you're actually burning up. It feels like—like you've got a real fever." Glancing to one side, she mumbled, "That's not supposed to happen."

"What?" I jerked to straighten up, the inklings of suspicion settling in. "What the hell is that supposed to mean? What have you done to me?"

Allie's gaze strayed over to my goblet of wine.

Oh, what the actual crap—

My eyes widened in fury. "Just what in the hell did you put in my drink?"

She threw her hands up awkwardly while at the same time trying to keep me upright. "I—I found some belladonna in the woods. I just wanted to put you to sleep so I can get the hell out of here. How was I supposed to know the herb would react badly with whatever you are?"

I clutched at my stomach. "Belladonna? Do you mean deadly nightshade?"

Her face fell. "Oh my god, are you dying?"

Before I could turn another exasperated glare onto her, the front door creaking open grabbed my attention.

Chez sauntered through with a confident pronouncement in the lilt of his tone. "The wildlings in the desert finally quieted down. I thought perhaps you were done seducing the girl—" The cat stopped short upon spotting us. "Oh, oops."

Allie hadn't noticed the door. More confused than startled, her eyebrows rose, her gaze darting around the loft in a puzzle even as she half-dragged me across the floor. "Who's seducing what now? Who said that?"

Chez pounced across the floor to settle upon the side table beside my bed. His big, yellow eyes stared up at the two of us as we got closer. "Hey, what the hell is going on here? Is Rabb hurt?"

Allie's eyes popped wider than the cat's. "Did that—? That cat just talked— Hey, did you just—?" Pausing, she shook her head briskly. "You know what, never mind. You, talking cat, can you help me with him?"

Licking one paw, Chez mewled. "Not really, since I seem to be a little bit cat-sized."

Lazy bastard. Rolling my eyes, I grunted as I was unceremoniously plopped onto my bed.

Allie grabbed a blanket and threw it over me. The surprise on her face morphed into derision. "Goodness, I have been petting you all week and you never mentioned that you could talk?"

"Who did you think I was talking to up here this whole time?" I prompted her in mocking.

"How the hell should I know?" Allie threw up her hands. "Nothing makes sense in this world. Well, I mean, I thought the weird forest of talking flowers and trees and caterpillars was just that." She cast a glance around the room. "What else talks in here? The furniture? The couch? The clock?"

"Just the cat," Chez replied coolly as he shifted to lounge on his back.

Allie blew out a breath as if to gain her bearings. "Then I suppose we haven't been formally introduced either." She read the name on his collar tag. "Chey?"

"No, no. Not Shay." Chez shook his head. "Chez, like Chezzzz, emphasize the Z. With a Zzz."

"Do you live here too?" Allie asked Chez.

"Absolutely not!" I managed to wheeze out first.

Allie was watching the stripes on Chez's fur coat change, the way his eyes occasionally spiraled purple. "He has such a weird grin."

Chez's grin widened. "That's because I'm a Cheshire cat."

"What does that mean?"

"It means...I'm a Cheshire cat. That's what it means."

Allie sighed. "Whatever. This world is odd. I can't even—" Hands on her hips, she shook her head at Chez. "So, are all animals in this world as eloquent as yourself?"

"Not as eloquent as myself, I should say." Chez's reply was a tad haughty. "But I do suppose it's more common than one might think. Even Rabb's animal form could speak."

Blinking in an indignant startle, I had to pointedly cut in, "Hey, that's none of her business—"

Allie's eyes were eagerly wide. "Rabb's got an animal form? What is it?"

Chez replied before I could stop him. "A little white rabbit."

"Ooh!" Allie cooed—she actually cooed.

I let out another exasperated groan of protest. "That was a long—I mean, I didn't—" I stopped short and slumped back in bed.

Allie was trying hard to bite back her laughter.

I glared at her yet again. "Oh, shut up."

Allie and Chez met each other's gazes and both of them burst out laughing.

I blinked hard. Seriously? What the hell were they doing making jokes when I could be dying?

"Oh, you know what—you two deserve each other." Grumbling, I tried to sit up in an attempt to get away from them but Allie shoved me back down.

"For god's sake, lie down." She put a hand on my forehead. "You're burning up."

I shrugged her hand off and turned away so my back was to her. "No, I'm not."

"Didn't you say you were the Queen of Hearts's most notorious assassin? How can you be such a big baby?"

"I'm not a—" I stopped short to cough, then I glanced back over my shoulder in incredulity. "Is nobody else alarmed that this girl just tried to poison me?"

Allie rolled her eyes. "Relax, if that herb was really going to kill you, you would be dead by now."

I shot her a suffering look. "Oh, I'm so relieved."

"Well, hey, you're the most powerful sorcerer in Wünder. Granting that condition is true, the conclusion must be that you're going to be fine. You probably just need some rest."

Chez gave her a curious look. "You say that with such conviction."

Allie shrugged. "It's only logical."

"What does logic have to do with it?" I snapped in annoyance. "You're a strange girl who doesn't belong here. You don't know anything. You don't even know anything about yourself."

"Tsk." Allie clicked her tongue. "I don't know if the cranky is him getting better or worse."

"His mystical core is sapped," Chez noted, looking me over. "Rabb just needs a moment to restore himself."

"Does he need any medicine? *Is* there any medicine in here?" Allie cast a glance around the loft.

"He's a sorcerer. The overnight mystic tides should restore his magic."

The rest of their conversation was hazy in my reverie as I slumped back against my pillow. My vision blurred. "Chez. Don't let her escape..."

5

Chapter Five - Allie's Lab

The overnight mystic tides regularly washed across the land, bringing fresh, renewed magic to all the creatures of Wünder. It was all I needed to regenerate my power core and recover from my sudden bizarre malady.

I was relieved to note that Allie was not in my loft when I awoke.

Chez was though.

The purple cat was lounging on the corner of my bed, licking one paw. When he noticed me stir, he shot me another big, yellow wide-eyed prompting look. "Sooo...the plan didn't work, huh?"

Groaning, I swung my legs over the side of the bed to sit up. I tilted my head at the faint clinking from the apartment beneath mine. "She's still here?"

Chez purred. "I guess she felt guilty for poisoning you."

I stared at the wooden floor panels. "She's a fool. She should have escaped when she had the chance."

Then again, there was no place in Wünder she could go where I couldn't track her down. Truth be told, I hadn't been on that kind of hunt in a while. Maybe I should have let her run.

It wasn't that taking lives ever made me feel anything. Not guilt. Not remorse. Not pleasure. It was just something I did. A finite order of steps.

I clutched at my chest—heavy today, and took several staggered deep breaths.

Perhaps I was also simply fooling myself. Perhaps Allie's heart wasn't a *coeur* at all. It was just an ordinary lump of worthless rock. And it was weighing me down.

A vision—a flash of large shadows looming over me accompanying an echo of screaming sent an unexpected twinge to my chest.

No. My gut told me I was right.

This heart held power.

This stolen heart in my chest was going to save me.

It had to save me.

I glanced up at the piles of books and papers on my desk to think back to my research. "Hey, Chez," I started. "Do you remember that odd heart a few decades ago in Ironhaven? Everyone thought it was empty too."

"Oh, yeah, that. People said it's because the lady was in some kind of accident and lost her memories." Chez shot me a look. "Do you think maybe that's the same case here?"

"Maybe." I nodded.

"And when the lady did recover her memories, her Heart-fire ember eventually came alive, right?" Chez asked.

I folded my hands together in deep thought. "The Queen scooped her up before word could spread, before anyone could figure it out. The sorcerer who claimed her has been long dead but..."

"The Duchess," Chez piped up.

"Yes." I nodded. The Duchess would have been involved in any heart harvesting across the land since even before I could remember. "If the Duchess can confirm the story, all we need to do is make sure the Queen doesn't catch this girl's scent until we can find a way to recover her memories," I proposed.

"She's a clever one, this." Chez gave me an eerie grin. "Last night, she told me she'd already been brainstorming a solution for that same thing all week. She reckons what she's building downstairs is the trick to getting back her memories and finding her way home."

I gave Chez an even glare. "I'm not letting that girl leave Wünder."

"Well, you don't have to tell her that," Chez pointed out. "All I'm saying is that since her goals are aligned with yours for the moment, perhaps it is in your best interests to help her with her mission. And if she succeeds, then you'll get what you want too."

I rubbed my chin in thought. "I suppose."

"Sooner rather than later. Like before Allie finds any more increasingly creative ways to escape. Or before either of you manage to kill the other." Chez's mischievous grin was bright yellow.

I glared at the cat. "This isn't funny, Chez."

"Agree to disagree, my friend," Chez bid before turning on his paws to leave. "Well, I suppose I should report back to the Duchess that the Queen of Hearts's most notorious assassin himself *wasn't* in fact assassinated last night."

Chez yowled, jumping away and out the door before I could kick him.

Although I trusted Chez well enough not to betray my confidence, the Duchess was perhaps the only other being on Wünder with whom this information was safe. She was like me in more ways than one.

I blew out an already exasperated breath before I stood up and made my way across my loft and down the spiral staircase.

I was of half a mind to reconsider and hit the books again, looking for another option, but I was already literally working against the clock.

My pocket watch indicated it was almost time to bring Allie's rations, but I wasn't particularly inclined to do her any favors.

Ducking my head as I descended the stairs, my eyes easily adjusted to the dim light.

Flickering gas lamps and the warm, amber glow of bulbs casting long shadows across the room, the storage studio beneath my loft seemed to have transformed into some kind of mad laboratory.

Set against the internal gears and cogs of the clock tower and walls lined with copper pipes and brass fixtures, the massive oak work table, which dominated the center of the small room, was cluttered with a small pile of papers, glassware, and some haphazardly arranged unidentifiable apparatus.

Allie had somehow collected an assortment of oddities, including smaller, intricately designed but broken-looking timepieces.

One side of the glassed-in clock tower mechanism was filled with chalky scribbles of complex equations, formulas, and sketches of a device, wherein several renditions of this device had been smudged or partially erased, mixed with elegant cursive and hurried scrawls.

I gawked. What the hell had she done to the place?

The entire room was filled with a constant low hum of machinery amidst the hollow ticking of the clock tower. A faint scent of oil and metal hung in the air.

Allie was busy—moving about the room with purpose, adjusting dials on a little rusty metal box, a machine of some type. Pencil in her hand, she scribbled something down on a half-crumpled scrap of paper on the table. Her lab coat was stained with various substances.

"What the hell is all this?"

Not startled by my proclamation in the least, she glanced up and incorrectly assumed that I was gesturing to the huge glass wall of scribbles and sketches. "I'm eliminating possibilities."

"No." I cleared my throat to amend. "What the hell is *all this*? Where did you find all this stuff?"

Her attention was still trained on the metal box as it softly whirred. "When was the last time you ventured downstairs? You didn't know that all eight stories below us in this creepy clock tower are a veritable gold mine of spare parts?"

I narrowed my eyes in mocking. "Everything I need is in

my loft upstairs. Why would I waste my time going down-stairs?"

"So much for pride in ownership," she mumbled.

I sniffed haughtily. "I don't own this clock tower. I merely live here."

She still barely looked up from reading her graphs, her tone as haggard as my own. "Why are you even down here? Look, if you've come to yell at me again, why not just write me a note? I promise I'll read it with a screamingly loud tone in my head."

Frowning, I couldn't seem to phrase in my head what I wanted to put across. I needed to help her? I *wanted* to help her? We needed to help each other? Every way I thought to say it sounded preposterous.

I pursed my lips. "I'm...looking for something."

"What? Attention? Still feverish?" She gestured offhand toward the messy single cot. "There's a blanket."

I followed her with an indignant gaze as she walked around me to peer out the tinted windows. Did she even forget that she was the reason I had succumbed to a staggering fever last night and nearly died? "Let me get this straight. I don't even get any sympathy?"

"Sympathy?"

"You tried to kill me last night!"

She rolled her eyes. "That was an accident." She looked me up and down and I belatedly realized I was standing in front of her workspace. "Can you—get out of the way, please?"

Annoyed I wasn't making any headway, I shot her another frown. Her entire aura was shooing me away. It was highly disconcerting. Normally, women couldn't get enough of my company. I had to remind myself again that, for whatever reason, my spells didn't work on Allie. I had to think of another way to get through to her. I clenched my fists in frustration.

Hearing my exasperated breath, perhaps the guilt finally caught up to her. "Look," Allie paused. "I am grateful that you saved my life and...let's suppose I was sorry for last night. But I have work to do. Needing to find a way home and whatnot."

"I know. That's why I'm here. It occurred to me—"

"It occurred to you...or Chez?" she interrupted with a knowing tone.

"Either way," I pressed, "it seems that our goals are aligned, and I believe it would be to our mutual benefit if we worked together."

Allie nodded as she pushed past me again. "Yeah, Chez totally thought of that."

I spun around to where she'd gone. "Whatever. The point is you would like to recover your memories. And I—" I broke off. There was no point explaining the entire situation to her, nor exposing the fact that whatever she remembered, whatever we discovered, she was still my prisoner. "Have a slightly related problem," I finished. "Therefore I have a proposal: I would be willing to offer you my help if you would be willing to cooperate with me. No doubt you must already realize that having the assistance of the most powerful sorcerer in the land would be to your benefit."

Allie's gaze was critical, clearly still suspicious. But after a moment, she conceded, "Fine. I guess two heads are always better than one."

Puzzled at her turn of phrase, I made a face. Since say,

for example, the creature you were fighting had two heads instead of one, your chances of prevailing would in fact be smaller. But I dismissed my query.

I cast a glance at the plethora of odd equipment Allie had set up on the work table. "So what exactly are you doing here?"

Allie's hazel eyes lit up. "I'm building a frequency detector. It compares the vibrations of one object against another. It's simple physics."

I wasn't expecting the depth of her answer. Her passion for her work was immediately clear in her voice, in her mere posture. "I thought you couldn't remember who you are. How do you know how to do all this?"

Allie shrugged, shoving her hands in the pockets of her lab coat. "I don't know. All of this stuff just seems to come easily to me."

I studied the wall of scribbles. "What kind of science is this?"

Her gaze followed mine. "Well, it looks like I dabble in many fields: materials science, mechanical engineering, chemistry...but it seems I specialize particularly in quantum physics and string theory."

I must have given her a blank look so she felt the need to elaborate—quite pointedly.

"Portals," she said, matter-of-factly. "Other dimensions. And I believe your world is one within which I have been inadvertently sucked into, somehow, for some reason."

I blinked, almost in ridicule. She had been saying as much. "Another world?"

"Yes."

I couldn't help making another face. "That sounds…"

"Mad?" she supplied. "Probably." There was a slight twinkle in her eye. "I have an idea. Let's do an experiment."

"An experiment?"

She nodded. "Yes. If we use the classic scientific method, we start with an observation. A question. Then we state our hypothesis. Then we do the procedure and analyze the data to formulate our conclusions." Her eyebrows rose in a prompt. "So let's suppose that everything from the same dimension vibrates with the same frequency—or at least they're supposed to."

She picked up one of the gadgets from the mess on the table. It was a long reed attached to a small bulb that glowed yellow at its end. She started pointing it around the room— for no reason that I could see since nothing was happening.

Wide-eyed, I wove away when she turned the stick toward me. "What are you doing?" I snapped one hand up as a reflex, ready to do a counterspell.

She chided, "Relax."

I looked from the stick to her and back. As far as I could see, still nothing had changed and nothing was happening. "What? Was something supposed to happen?"

She bit her lip before she turned the stick inward to point at herself.

My eyes widened when the bulb at the end began to glow a smoky green hue.

Allie seemed to release the breath she was holding before hastily setting the stick back down on the table. The light in the bulb fizzled out in a puff of smoke.

Her tone sombered at her conclusion. "Figured." She took

a deep breath and began again, "Under certain conditions, empty space might contain vibratory discrepancies. These are spots where the barriers between places are thinner. I have a feeling if I test the hollow in the tree leading to Tulgey Woods, I'll find the same thing." She drew another wooden stick from a pile beside her as if to start again. "That means all I need to do is find an intersect, a convergence significant enough—a tunnel, a doorway if you will." Her eyes shone with determination. "And once I do, I'm sure I'll find a portal that leads all the way home. It's the only plausible explanation."

The light in her eyes dimmed as she finished as though she was spent from her tirade. Her shoulders slumping, Allie braced one hand against the table.

From my magical perception, Allie's aura flickered and dimmed.

Was she getting sick now too? Curling my fingers, I cast a spell and a thin veil of fog covered Allie for a moment so I could assess her physical condition.

I frowned again. She was fatigued, dehydrated. She must have soldiered on through the night. Perhaps with doing all of this work, she was as exhausted as I was.

"Here." I snapped my fingers to conjure a glass of water. "You look tired. You should probably lie down."

"Did you poison this?" Allie eyed the glass in my hand. "Why are you suddenly being so nice to me?"

I rolled my eyes. "Cut the crap. Just drink it."

Her lips curled in a pout of protest but she took the glass from me, took a big swig, paused for a moment as if to make sure she didn't keel over straight away, and then swallowed. "Thank you."

Fidgeting in my stance, I cleared my throat. "You should rest."

"I'm fine. I just need to take deep breaths." Then her eyes narrowed in suspicion as she straightened up again. "You're not still trying to seduce me, are you?"

I wrinkled my nose in disdain. "Trust me. I'm definitely not."

"Well, good." She nodded approval before shrugging off-handedly. "I don't think I can fall in love anyway. At least not like normal people do."

I mocked, "Are you not 'normal people'?"

"I'm a genius." Her answer seemed like a reflex response.

Her response fell into the silence as I kept her gaze but she didn't seem to want to look away.

A faint keening caught my ears.

I almost ignored it. But in the next moment, a tiny fragment of a spark flared from the work table.

Eyes widening, I didn't stop to think before I lunged to grab Allie and hauled us both to the floor as a flash of light accompanied a BOOM!

I cocooned her in my arms as we landed on the floor with a hard thump.

Scrap paper, sawdust, and shards of glass pattered down like rain for a few long moments.

When the only sound around us had reverted to the lone ticking of my clock, Allie met my just-as-stunned gaze through the lingering smoke as she panted beneath me. None too casually, she blew her disheveled hair out of her face. "Holy crap, that was close."

I pushed up on my arms above her. "What the hell was

that?" I yelled in her face. "Are you working with explosives down here? Do you realize what could have happened if that had blown up in your face? What else are you even working on?"

Sitting up to dust herself off, Allie made a face. "Those were probably just the volatile chemicals I mixed by accident. What is the big deal? All experiments come with their own set of risks."

Rage nearly burst out of my chest. The stupid, stubborn girl didn't even realize what could have happened!

I jumped to straighten up with a growl. "This is totally unacceptable."

I waved one hand, and in a blink, the condition of the cramped studio returned to its original state. A dusty boiler sat across a modest but neatly made bed in the sparsely furnished space, amidst the backdrop of the inner workings of the giant timepiece visibly moving in a mechanic rhythm in tune to the hollow echoes of the ticking clock, and all of Allie's scribblings and whatever equipment she had lugged in there disappeared.

Allie threw up her arms in indignant complaint. "What the—? Where's all my stuff?"

I moved to stalk away.

She called out after me, "Hey! I thought we agreed we were going to cooperate with each other?"

"By that, I meant *I* will come up with a plan and you will follow my instructions," I corrected. "Did you forget I needed you alive?" I gave her another glare. "I can't have you toying around with any of this dangerous science nonsense. I forbid it."

"You forbid it?" Allie echoed in incredulity. "You're such a jerk!"

Ignoring her attempt to give chase, I whirled on my heel and apparated away with a poof.

6

Chapter Six - The
Bad Guy

Chez was crazy to suggest that I cooperate with that strange girl.

In all my centuries of existence, I had always worked alone. Always.

The incident with the explosion was my punishment for thinking otherwise.

I didn't need anyone else's help. Besides, normal humans were incredibly fickle creatures. Not to mention all their capacity for any action would always be hindered by emotions. Such things made one weak.

I clutched at my chest again.

The heart inside me was full of disquiet. It was making me even more tetchy than usual. Notwithstanding the more frequent bouts of anger, I was beginning to succumb to mood swings, finding it difficult to concentrate on my work—on anything. Adding fuel to the fire, my temperament was getting so volatile that it was no longer practical to receive any more companions.

Allie had also been making it a point to ignore me altogether. She wouldn't touch her trays of food. She would sulkily work through the night with her noisy machines and loud banging.

I needed to get rid of her so badly.

If there was ever any argument for how emotions incapacitated power, it was this. Me. Right this moment.

I sensed the cat's presence before I heard the mewl as Chez padded through the doorway as it shut behind him with a clang.

Tossing back the last of my wine, I pushed my chair back.

Chez's giant yellow eyes met mine—sober, unlike usual. "It's time again."

I nodded once. "I know."

The cat hopped up to the back of the couch beside me so I could unlatch a rolled-up scroll attached to his collar.

With a flick of my hand and a spell, the scroll floated in mid-air, and, amidst a golden haze, unrolled itself.

I almost didn't need to read it all the way through.

The Queen of Hearts's seal was blood red on the bottom.

Regardless of my unstable condition, potentially waning magic, personal problems, and whatnot, I couldn't ignore the Queen's bidding. The Queen still needed to eat. And I needed to hunt.

After a moment, the scrap of paper ignited into a small fireball, hefting it up into the air; the fire consuming the note like a greedy ghost as the leftover ashes disappeared into the ether.

I pursed my lips. "The Queen wants to take Veridia."

"The next mission is a target? Not a hunt?" Chez mused. "The Queen hasn't asked you to do one in a while. There must be a really big threat."

I stood up to get ready. "The kingdom of Veridia has been a hold-out for decades. They've never recognized the Queen's authority. Plus Veridia's princess is expected to wed into another powerful family and there have been rumors that they are growing in strength and support. This union would make them even stronger."

"A wedding? Ouch. Two strikes. Is this princess deliriously happy? We all know the Queen can't stand that." Chez stretched out on my desk. "Well, Her Majesty has already heard about this one so you can't delay."

I took the other trinket dangling from his collar and stared at it for a moment. If only the *coeur* burned, I could capture it right now. Shaking my head, I pocketed the miniature Heartlamp. "I know my job, Chez."

Hearing rustling from the studio downstairs, Chez quirked his head. "What are you going to do about Allie?"

I groaned at the mention of her name. I didn't want to be bothered with her for now. She just needed to stay the hell out of trouble.

I gave Chez a pointed look. "Do you think you can keep her here?"

"Sure. We'll play Parcheesi. Where do you keep the board games?"

Ignoring Chez's snide comment, I merely shook my head before disappearing with my usual burst of smoke.

The Kingdom of Veridia was perched atop a rugged mountain peak. Its thick stone walls seamlessly integrated with intricate brass and copper embellishments as steam billowed from vents placed along the castle's exterior, blending with the mountain mist.

It might have been beautiful. But, to me, it was just another kingdom. Just another target. Just another day.

As I coasted closer, high in the air, the royal courtyard's embellishments appeared even grander. Tables draped in rich fabrics were set with exquisite center pieces and floral arrangements, and brass lanterns emitted a gentle steam-infused glow, as the bride and groom stood at the top of the wide aisle laden with rose petals, big, joyous smiles on their faces.

Blissful.

Oblivious.

Unaware.

Honestly, they should have seen this coming.

Seen *me* coming.

All the kingdoms in Wünder, no matter how powerful, how innovative, how unique, would always succumb to the Queen of Hearts. No attempts to overthrow the Queen in the past had ever succeeded. And they never ever would.

Because of me.

As I rode in on a dark cloud, the sky lit up with lightning

and I grabbed the bride. She screamed as we lifted into the air, her struggle against my grasp futile.

All at once, a barrage of arrows and swords and magic came whizzing right at me from all directions but I barely needed to wave my arm to summon a thick fog that disabled them and enveloped the entire kingdom. A fresh surge of energy boosting my powers, everything seemed easier today.

So easy.

With another wave of my arm, multiple copies of myself set upon to attack the rest of the guests and guards in the courtyard, in barely visible shadowy blurs, bathing the air in horrified screams, slashing, breaking, and generic terror.

Just another day. Just another—

A deep stabbing in my chest caused me to suck in a gasp.

What—

Blinking, I cast a confused look around but the princess and I were all alone, aloft in the air. There was no culprit. No enemy. No dagger. No arrow. I glanced down at my shirtfront. No crimson stain. No wound. No visible injury.

Except for this agonizing sensation of gouging pain in the core of my body.

Swallowing hard, my eyes widened in almost knowing dread, as suddenly—the supposedly lifeless heart in my chest began to beat...

Hard.

Strong.

Fast.

I groaned at the sting, almost dropping the princess of Veridia in my shock. Although, perhaps I should have. Her screams were grating in my ears.

But dammit—what the actual hell was going on?

I forced a couple of blinks and an overwhelming wave of force struck me, a concussive impact like a physical blow, and a momentary burst of light seared my eyes.

When I opened my eyes again, for some reason I was seeing the world as though I was outside myself.

I realized exactly what was going on.

Allie.

Allie was here.

And more than feeling her feelings, this time, I could see what she was seeing.

From some dark corner of the courtyard, Allie was watching the dozens of copies of the monstrous sorcerer decimate all the guests at the wedding, blood spraying everywhere as I whirled in the air, on the ground, and in between tables as I attacked everyone.

Allie's heart hammered even harder in my chest.

The princess's screams rang in the air as I slaughtered each and every one of her loved ones. At the same time, the accumulated mystical power contained in her heart grew and grew, because the more of her loved ones I slew, the more powerful her heart was going to be once harvested.

When the last of her family was slain, I, the monster, reached into the princess's chest and extracted her still-beating heart. With its substantial power, it glowed in my hand, ever so much more than the last ember I had collected.

As I slowly descended to the courtyard, my feet touching down on the floor, my vision returned to me.

The princess of Veridia went slack in my grasp. She crumpled to the stone floor to her knees.

Her mouth still open in silent horror, the princess lifted her wide eyes to me, as if to watch as I drew something from my pocket. With another spell of my finger, the little trinket from Chez grew into a full-sized Heartlamp.

I slipped the glowing heart ember within the glass containment and the princess of Veridia's eyes rolled into the back of her head. Her face turned ashen. Her body fell limp to one side—lifeless.

On cue, all the ghostly instances of myself vanished with a poof into the carpet of gray fog that remained around us.

I took a deep breath.

Mission accomplished.

Taking a moment, I clenched my teeth to rein in the initial shock at the overwhelming feelings I'd felt from Allie. The rapid beating of the heart in my chest turned from incredibly alarming to merely disconcerting.

Cracking my neck in the strain, I strode across the courtyard.

Allie was crouched beside one of the marble balustrades. Her eyes were wide, her face pale.

All around us, wildfires still crackled, smoke and fog lacing the chilly night with a ruinous omen, the flickering fire the only glow in the darkness, but the courtyard and the kingdom had gone otherwise silent.

Because I had killed everyone.

As I approached Allie, the heart in my chest beat a bit faster again, accompanied by a heavy dread. There was a sinking feeling in my stomach, as though every hair on my body stood on end, every nerve was alert, alarmed. My mouth was dry. My skin cold.

I tilted my head.

Was this...fear?

I let out a slow breath.

I was feeling Allie's fear.

I hadn't felt fear in a long, long time.

The vision of those terrifying shadows came screaming back into my mind. I couldn't move. Instead of Allie, it was me crouched low on the ground, my head covered with my arms. I didn't want to see. I didn't want to hear. I didn't want to feel...

I forcibly shook my head to clear the disturbing images.

Not now.

Steadying myself, I held my hand out to help Allie up. "Come, we must return to my tower."

Allie's face was blank. It was as if her brain had churned to a halt after attempting to process too many thoughts. Her voice was flat when she asked, "What-what are you?"

I cleared my throat. "I told you. I am the Queen of Hearts's most notorious assassin."

Her expression didn't change. "You're...the bad guy."

I sniffed. Well, at least now perhaps she finally believed how powerful I really was.

She extended a finger toward the object in my hand. "And what-what is that?"

"It's called a Heartlamp."

"You killed everyone. And you...stole her heart."

"That is my job. The Queen of Hearts tasks me to fetch fresh hearts for her to eat."

"Eat?"

"In a manner of speaking. Hearts contain powerful mystical

energy. I bring the Queen the hearts and she extracts their energy magic."

Allie clutched at her chest. "I had a feeling... I couldn't feel mine..." Her tone hollowed. "Did you give my heart to the Queen too? How am I still alive?"

"You're lucky. You are too weird for me to give your heart over to the Queen. But hers..." I lifted the Heartlamp in a gesture, referring to the heart from the princess of Veridia. "Will make the Queen even more powerful than she already is."

Her forehead creased. "So, my heart is...?"

"Here." I tapped my chest. "Outside a body, without a Heartlamp, your heart would have withered away."

Allie's chest began to heave, like she already knew the answer to her next question, but knew she still must ask it. She swallowed hard. "Are you...going to give me my heart back?"

"No," I replied clearly, meeting her watery gaze steadily. "It's mine. Like I told you. You are mine now."

7

Chapter Seven - Shadows

I didn't sleep well.

I knew Allie was plagued with nightmares all night—and therefore so was I.

Visions of the monster decimating all the wedding guests, the terrified screams, the spray of blood, and the stench of death haunted her dreams.

Understandably.

However, this morning, the beating of the heart in my chest had gone back to a normal, steady pace. Clutching at my shirtfront, I took a deep breath to steel myself. It was quite a disconcerting sensation after centuries of nothing, of hollowness.

But all this confusion would soon end, I assured myself. I just had to endure a little bit longer and then I would get what I wanted.

As I sat on my bed to catch my breath, I tilted my head to

one side at a faint noise. I looked around my silent loft and easily concluded that the noise was coming from downstairs.

Of course, it was.

With an exasperated grumble, I pushed up to stalk down the spiral staircase to check up on what the hell Allie was up to.

Was she trying to escape again? I wouldn't have blamed her.

Halfway down the stairs, I blinked in surprise.

Allie had somehow resurrected many of the things I had magically whisked away. Her gaze was newly determined as she worked.

I didn't sense any hint of fear or anxiety in her person.

Until she looked up and spotted me coming down.

But even then, her fear this morning was muted.

It was as though she'd had time to think, to calm down, to rationalize overnight.

Tilting my head, I assessed her aura once more. It was in neither of our interests if she got sick or became distraught from apprehension.

I had to clear the air first. "You weren't supposed to be there."

Not meeting my gaze, Allie shook her head.

"How did you even follow me?" I wanted to know.

"I jumped into your portal wake."

"My...what?"

She pressed her lips together. "I was...eavesdropping. Again. When you were talking to Chez." Her gaze dropped. "I saw you as you were about to leave for your mission. I don't know why I thought it could work, but I jumped into the space you teleported through, and then I found myself where you were."

My blood running cold, I clenched my jaw. "You did...what?"

"I was curious."

My eyebrows snapped together in a nearly uncontrollable rage. What the damn hell—was she actually crazy? I surged forward. "You—have no idea how dangerous that was—what you'd done! You can't always guarantee where those things lead. Who knows where you could have ended up?"

I suppressed the urge to throttle her, taking another step closer, making Allie stumble. She backed up until she was pressed against the glass wall. The giant exposed brass gears within the tower chugged mechanically behind her, the weights and chains pulling and shifting as the witness clock ticked and tocked.

A rumble of clouds mirrored in Allie's wide eyes as my darkness descended into the room, almost blocking out the light from the windows, snuffing out the lamp lights on the table, rendering the space close to pitch black.

With a grave, menacing look, I caged her in with my body and bent my head even closer to rasp the words in her face. "Swear to me you won't ever do that again."

Unwilling to meet my cold gaze, hers was off to one side but she managed the words, "I-I swear."

Vindicated, I couldn't help a slight smirk. "Are you afraid of me now?"

Allie still wouldn't meet my gaze.

That should have been my answer.

But for some reason, I wanted her to say it.

"Allie?" I prompted.

Swallowing hard, Allie shook her head. "I'm not afraid of you." She looked up to meet my gaze evenly. "I'm not, Rabb."

Unbidden, my dark clouds began to recede. What? "I've just told you I kill people and harvest their hearts. You already know I've done the same to you. I have your heart trapped. I hold you hostage. Even if you escape or try to run away again, I will always find you. You're not afraid?"

She took a deep breath. "You haven't hurt me yet. On the contrary, you've taken really good care of me so far."

I met her gaze with a sneer, trying to will my terrifying shadows back. "I've told you I need you alive. It has nothing to do with taking care of you."

Still, she shrugged. "I'm a scientist. All I know is the proof I have."

Whether she was just saying it to put on a brave front, put me off-balance, or she really believed it, it was a futile thing to threaten someone who wasn't at all frightened. I almost groaned in annoyance. I couldn't seduce her. I couldn't scare her. Did nothing I do affect her at all?

A bit confused and disoriented, I stepped back enough to give her space to breathe, the light in the room returning as the fog lifted.

I was at an absolute total loss for what to do.

Allie shifted in her stance. "Can I...ask you a question?"

I narrowed my eyes at her instead of responding.

She asked anyway, "Do—do you feel guilty at all? About what you just did?"

I sniffed. "I cannot feel guilt or remorse. Those feelings, those weak human feelings, have long been removed from me."

"You...basically just massacred an entire kingdom, maybe even two," she pointed out. "You don't even feel bad in the least? Don't you worry about—" She rolled her shoulders. "I don't know, karma?"

Not understanding, I quirked my head.

"You know..." She threw her hands up. "Your comeuppance. The part where you get what you deserve in the end."

Not defensive in the slightest, I folded my arms across my chest. "My soul has been black from the beginning. This is what I was made for."

I had certainly never suffered anything untoward despite every wicked command of the Queen's I had carried out. I remembered every horrible thing I had ever done. I had never once had to consider the consequences of my actions. It was my job. My sole purpose.

Nothing else mattered save for the clock to keep ticking.

Allie bit her lip. "Can I ask you another question?"

She probably had about a million questions by now. "What?"

Allie was staring intently at my chest. "If you carry mine in there, where is *your* heart?"

I shrugged. "I don't know. I don't think I ever had one. Or if I did, it's been lost a while."

Her one eyebrow quirked up. "You don't want to find it?"

"I've never needed a heart to live." Nonchalantly, I turned away. "I know I'm a monster."

"The Queen is a monster," Allie corrected. "For making you do this. She's manipulating you for her own gains..." Her forehead creased as if in an inkling of a recollection and a dark shadow crossed her face. "I think...maybe I might have also done something like that."

On the brink of eagerness and anticipation, my eyes widened. "Are you starting to remember something about who you are?"

She dropped her gaze. "I have a feeling I was not truly good either."

I studied her face, waiting to see if she remembered anything else. If she did, then perhaps all my troubles could be over as soon as today.

A brief streak of sunlight slipped through the clouds, filtering in through the windows, but the momentary glimmer of a trance on her face passed just as quickly.

Pursing my lips, I straightened up. I supposed I shouldn't have expected it was going to be that easy.

Allie dropped her gaze. Her thoughts had visibly shifted. I could almost see the gears in her mind turning. "That girl, last night—she...died when you put her heart in that thingy."

I nodded. "Yes."

"But *I* didn't die when you took mine," she noted.

"They don't always die," I dismissed since I couldn't explain any further.

All these centuries of doing this, it had never once occurred to me to ask how exactly a Heartlamp functioned. And why should it? Such details were irrelevant to my job.

I tapped my chest, gesturing between us. "Besides, you might have noticed. One doesn't always need a heart to survive in Wünder."

Allie's eyes narrowed. Her busybody brain was working on something. "Right. So the fact of the matter is...you don't really need me. For some reason, you just need my heart. And I could go on happily existing even without it."

I quirked an eyebrow. "I wouldn't say 'happily'. You should have lost all your emotions." Or *at least* she should have.

I knew this much for a fact. Wünder had a certain population of people wandering around, sallow and stripped of feelings, many of them victims of my services. These people moved through their day-to-day like ghosts haunting their villages. They may as well have been ghosts.

But for reasons I was cautious to admit even to myself, Allie, of course, was nothing like them.

"What?" I prompted, my tone lowering half in dread. I wasn't sure if I ought to be worried or not about Allie's slow nodding as she processed this information.

"The other day, you offered to help me." Allie met my gaze. "I have a counteroffer. An exchange. You help me find a way home and in return, you can keep my heart. I mean, all the evidence suggests you don't really need me—at least, not *me* in particular."

I sneered again. "I already have your heart. I own you. You have no leeway for negotiation, no leverage."

Allie narrowed her eyes. "But I have a distinct feeling you're as eager to get my heart out of you as I am to get home. And if you haven't ripped it out of your chest just yet, I'm sure there is a reason. Given what you are, and having observed your behavior for the last few weeks, I even deduce that it's actually detrimental to you to have a real heart after all these years. Ergo, I will help you with what you need if you help me with what I need."

I blinked at her unexpected insights.

Damn, this girl was clever.

"And if we don't find you a way home?" I quirked an eyebrow.

"Well, then that is my risk to take." She nodded solemnly. "Do we have a deal?"

"What if I don't accept your offer?"

"Then-then I'll be relentless." She stuck her chin up. "I already know, for some reason, you aren't able to kill me—maybe you can't or just don't want to. I'll try to escape every day and get into all the trouble I can find. Either way, you'll never get a moment's peace."

My eyes flashed. "Look, you—" But I stopped short when something clicked in my mind.

Allie didn't know what the Duchess's job was. She didn't know how the Heartlamp worked either. She didn't have the faintest idea about magic or how Heartfire embers were used in Wünder. This was something I could use to my advantage.

I folded my arms across my chest. "Fine. Have it your way."

Allie narrowed her gaze at me in suspicion.

Drat. Perhaps I had agreed too quickly.

She peered at my face. "How do I know I can trust you to keep your word?"

Giving her an even glare back, I measured my words carefully. "I assure you I have no interest in keeping you around. You were right in what you said before. I am as eager to get this heart out of me as you are to get home. I promise you we will both get what we want."

Satisfied with that, Allie nodded. "Fine. First things first. I need to get my memories back. The other day, you seemed to have an idea how to go about retrieving them."

I cleared my throat. Starting again, I tried to make my tone as guileless as possible. "I mean there have been stories of a similar case like yours. I believe there is a way to restore your memories."

She tapped her chin. "What did you call that thing where you put the girl's heart again?"

"A Heartlamp. It is the only vessel that can contain a Heartfire ember."

I had to control the eagerness in my tone. If I could convince her to go see the Duchess... That was, if I could convince Allie to willingly deposit her Heartfire ember in a Heartlamp then perhaps I would get what I want. And once the power of her heart was extracted, Allie would no longer be my problem.

Careful not to let anything slip, I tilted my head as I spoke. "The Duchess is the only being on Wünder who makes the Heartlamps. I think if we could get the Duchess to craft you a special Heartlamp, it might help unblock your memories and you'll remember who you are."

Allie's response was a slow nod.

I shrugged. "I mean, I won't have the faintest clue how to find your way home back to...wherever you're from. I'll not be able to help you there."

"I know. Leave that to me." She gestured to her work table. "I've been working on an experiment that should help me find a way home. In fact, I was very close before you magicked away all my stuff." She waved her hand as if mimicking what I'd done. "I found replacement parts for most of the things you threw away. Can you get them back?"

I gave her a no-nonsense look. No.

She rolled her eyes. "Fine. I guess I'll have to make do."

A meowing near the stairs caught her attention as Chez padded down the spiral steps.

"Chez!" Allie broke into a smile.

Chez pounced along and jumped up to the table beside Allie. "I brought you a gift."

Allie plucked a small metal item from the purple cat's collar. Her eyes widened in pleasure. "This is great, Chez. It's the last thing I need to make another frequency detector. Thank you so much!"

I glanced from one to the other. I could care less about their tedious exchanges.

"How are you doing, Allie?" Chez asked, his tone adopting concern.

"Okay, I guess." Allie shrugged as she spun to settle in her seat. "I still keep thinking this is all just a dream and that I will soon wake up, safe in my bed. But I guess...there goes that theory." She drew out a few tools and scattered certain things before her. "The good news is Rabb has agreed to help me with my mission."

"Did he now?" Chez looked amused, if not in disbelief.

I gave Chez a pointed look. "I told Allie we need another Heartlamp that only your mistress, the Duchess makes. She makes all the mystical Heartlamps for the Queen. We'll need her to make another one for yours. And once you've deposited your heart in the Heartlamp, you'll definitely regain your memories." I raised an eyebrow, almost daring him to contradict me. "Isn't that right, Chez?"

Chez looked puzzled for a moment before he caught on. "Oh—oh yeah, right. That's definitely something that's very possible. The Duchess can definitely help you with that." He rolled over on the table, stretching out. "Besides that, I mean that heart really shouldn't be inside you, Rabb. It's just...off-putting."

Allie's forehead creased in curiosity as she met my gaze. "Why didn't you have a new Heartlamp made before?"

I shot her a pointed look. "I haven't told anyone about this, Allie. About you. If anyone finds out I'm keeping a—" *coeur*, I almost said before stopping short to amend, "your heart, we'll both be in grave danger."

"Perfect." Allie pounded the table with her fist in enthusiasm. "Then there's only one thing to do. Let's go see this Duchess."

Chez tilted his head to look at me. "You know you're going to have to cross the River of Tears, right?"

I resisted the urge to groan. "I know."

Chez's eyebrows shot up. "Okay. Wow."

Allie looked from me to the cat and back again. "Is that a big deal?"

Wordless, I averted my gaze.

"Rabb hates that river. He hasn't been across it in decades," Chez relayed. "The River is...dangerous for people like him."

"Dangerous how?"

"Magic doesn't work there. Rabb will be powerless."

Allie's mouth formed an 'o' in acknowledgment.

Chez went on, "There's a man they call The Dodo. He's a slimy, unscrupulous fellow, runs a gambling den on a steamboat that cruises up and down the river." He tiled his head to point out, "Only way to ensure no cheating is not to have magic. It's the only place gambling thrives. He's carved out quite the market for himself. Of course, the house takes a cut off the top of all earnings, so really, the only winner is The Dodo."

Her attention now back on her work, Allie merely nodded. "Sounds logical."

Chez chuckled. "I knew I liked her." He cast me a glance. "Rabb, doesn't Allie just glow with such...an ominous positivity?"

I huffed and whirled around to make my leave.

From behind me, sparks lit up the room as Allie soldered something on her work table and a rusty tang tickled my nose.

I glanced back to see Allie blow the dust and smoke from the object on the table before picking it up. I narrowed my eyes at the yellowish orb hanging on a chain as Allie drew it around her neck.

"So," Allie started to Chez. "This scary Queen of yours. She sounds quite gruesome."

"Yeah, she eats all the hearts she can get her hands on. Nobody escapes that."

"Except me," she quipped.

"Well, we'll hope so."

I turned to climb back up the stairs but I couldn't help but dally near the top so I could eavesdrop on the rest of their conversation.

"Chez?"

"What?"

"Why can't Rabb give my heart to the Queen?"

"I told you, it's a weird one."

"Weird how?"

"It's empty, for starters."

"Because I lost my memories?"

"Probably," Chez relayed. "Most hearts hold fond memories of loved ones in them. It's part of what attributes the power. Do you remember anyone you loved?"

Allie's gaze glazed over. "I think… I think I may have loved someone. But I don't remember." She fiddled with her fingers as if straining to remember before blowing out a resigned breath. "What do you suggest I do now, Chez?"

The cat shrugged—in as much as a cat could shrug. He gave her a pointed look before responding, "I say…follow the white rabbit."

8

Chapter Eight - Caucus

Coming to land on a small meadow hilltop along the river, I dropped Allie unceremoniously to her feet.

She nearly stumbled. "Ow, thanks a lot," she muttered. "Just so you know, I'm not a big fan of being carried around like a damsel in distress."

I rolled my eyes. "I told you, I can only teleport across the realm by myself, and—" I paused to pointedly remind her, "you said you didn't want me to shrink you and carry you in my pocket."

"Fine." Straightening up, she brushed off her lab coat. "So if there's no magic on the river, how exactly are we going to get to the Duchess if you can't fly me across either?"

I jerked my thumb backward.

Behind us, past a modest pumpkin patch and an eerie scarecrow wearing an odd flat cap, the lane carved on the grass led to a weathered wooden jetty that was bobbing on the water.

A rhythmic chugging turned Allie's head as a plume of steam billowed from across the way and a water vessel materialized from a mystical mist.

Despite its puffing smokestacks, the riverboat's most prominent features were the wooden paddle wheels mounted on both sides and the grand paddle wheel at the stern churning water in its wake, propelling the vessel through the river.

Its multi-deck exterior with a tiered promenade was wrapped in intricate wrought-iron railings around an elegant hull with gold accents and decorative trim. Upper decks with arched windows were framed by elaborate curtains and lace.

The vessel's name was painted along its side.

Caucus.

Allie's eyes were wide in wonder.

Checking my pocket watch for the time, I pursed my lips. "As soon as we step foot on that boat, my magic will stop working, which opens us up to a significant measure of danger."

Her curious gaze turned up to meet mine. "Why? Do you owe this Dodo guy money?"

"I've stolen the hearts of many of his women and several of his men's wives," I relayed offhandedly.

Allie's eyes bulged. "What? Jeez, everyone will recognize you!" She smacked her palm against her forehead. "What was I thinking? Of course! You're the Queen's henchman. Everyone hates you."

I barely winced. "Hates me? Fears me, more like."

She made a face. "Whatever you want to call it. Either way,

it looks like we'll need to go in disguise." She cast a glance up and down my form and waved her arm. "Come on, give me your cloak." Digging in her pockets, she fished out a few things to hand to me—an elastic band and a pair of glasses. "Tie up your hair and wear these."

I stepped back. "No."

Groaning out loud, she tugged on my arm and quite forcibly dragged my cloak off me. "Hey—!" Before I could finish my protest, with a swish, Allie had wrapped the distinctive cloak around her waist like a skirt, before tucking the orb necklace into her shirt as though to hide it.

"Do you want to cross the river or not?" Allie went on with a grumble as she pulled me down the lane. Then grabbing the hat off the scarecrow, she stuck it onto my head.

Indignation rising in my chest, I could only sneer at her.

I hated this.

I had to do this.

She held out the elastic band and glasses to me again.

Groaning out loud in exasperation, I shrugged out of her grasp to comply. The rubber band pulled at my hair and the glasses blurred nearly everything in my view. I slid them half-way down the bridge of my nose so I could at least still see properly.

"There." She nodded after a moment, tilting her head to appraise my appearance. "You almost look like a regular, powerless guy—and much less likely to get us both killed." With her grasp firm on my arm, Allie half-dragged me toward the boarding platform. "Now come on before we miss the boat."

The whistle blew, signaling cast off just as we walked past the ramp to come on board.

As we headed straight into the parlor, I was hoping the colorful, likely highly inebriated crowds would lend to our disguises.

The blustery draft shoving us through the doorway blew Allie's hair across her face. In an almost futile effort, she tucked it back behind her ear before glancing back at me. "This place is amazing." She marveled at the lavish interior of plush velvet furnishings, polished wood paneling, and brass fittings.

Her forehead creased as her eyes kept catching on the people milling around us. "Are...they all animals?" Her question was full of wonder as we walked past a gentleman with horns like a rhino wearing a three-piece suit and boutonniere. On the small red-velvet curtained stage off to the left, three ladies in pink sashes with long thin legs and slender, curved beaks in place of mouths, were dancing the Can-Can to a merry tune.

I didn't bother answering her ridiculous question. Of course, they were all animals. On the river with no magic, certain creatures of Wünder could opt to mimic the human form. How else would they be able to gamble?

Allie wasn't waiting for my response. Distracted by something else, she surged forward through the main deck.

I followed in her wake, glancing past the open doors to one side that led to the casino.

Despite it being midday, the air in the casino was thick with cigar smoke, the clinking of poker chips and shuffling of cards on polished mahogany tables, and the constant hum of conversation.

"Ooh...can we check out the casino later?" Her eyes

widened again when her gaze landed on a set of long tables laden with food—fresh, shiny fruits and vegetables, glistening silver platters, and decadent cakes. "Oh my gosh, there's a snack bar! Look!" She made a beeline for the buffet and before I could even remind her that we were supposed to keep a low profile, she was already helping herself and loading a plate.

I had to roll my eyes as Allie made a face to pick out some tomatoes from her plate. What was she even doing? She'd said everything in this world tasted like waffles anyway. I didn't understand her urge to be picky. But I didn't bother to ask.

"Hello."

The soft purr at my elbow made me turn.

A woman dressed in bird feathers was gazing up at me with doe eyes behind her lory mask. Her smile glistened as she cooed, her voice dripping with honey. "Darling, would you like to buy me a drink?"

I blew out a tired breath. "No, thank you."

I certainly didn't mean for my voice to be husky or inviting at all but just then two more women in aviary costumes behind Miss Lory turned at the sound and two more breathy hellos came my way.

This.

This was what was supposed to happen.

I didn't even have any magic. I'd barely even done anything. And I was already about to be mobbed by women on this friggin' boat.

Another woman dressed all in canary yellow from clear across the room caught my eye and she began to walk over, prompting several other women to turn to look—at me.

Holding her plate under her chin so as not to spill, Allie's face was crumpled up as she watched the oddity happening around us. "What the hell is going on?" she mumbled through her mouthful.

"I think if we would like to remain incognito, you'd better put that plate down." I pulled on her arm to hurry away.

"Mm—!" She moaned in protest as I led her away but not before grabbing a few muffins to stuff in her pockets.

Fast-walking down the aisle, we headed down the stairs and turned into a narrow corridor near the cabins below deck before I glanced back to check if we were still being followed. Usually, once I'd moved out of immediate vicinity, the haze on these women would be lifted. It wasn't always a guarantee but it was as much as I could do on a moving boat.

Allie couldn't stifle her laughter any longer. Her hand propped against the wall to steady herself, she bent over to crack up. "What—the hell was that?"

I scoffed. I couldn't think how to explain it to her since she wasn't in the least affected by my influence. "Never mind," I dismissed. "We just have to lay low until the boat docks. Avoid The Dodo and his men. And avoid any women."

"That's just great." Allie frowned, casting a glance around the cramped, dark hallways below deck. "This is going to be one exciting boat ride."

A cackle of female laughter rang out from quite close by and I stiffened in wariness but the corridor was still deserted.

Allie craned her neck to look around. "Must be coming from the people in these cabins." She moved down the hall, running her fingers across the polished wood.

A click from the next door made her freeze in her tracks. Someone was coming out.

Backing up, Allie bumped into me. With another glance around, she pushed me into the gap between a cabin and the closed hatch before I could offer a dispute.

Slurs and giggling passed us by. Footsteps clomped up the stairs before becoming faint.

Allie craned her neck over her shoulder to check if the coast was clear before letting out a sigh. "That was close."

I glared down at her in displeasure. Her hand was clutched at my shirt as she pressed me back against the wall. "Get off of me."

She met my gaze in ridicule. "Calm down. Or maybe you want to get pawed by those women again?"

I gritted my teeth, ready with my rant. "Those women—"

Another shuffling came from down the hall and Allie jumped to cover my mouth with her hand.

This time, low, deep voices were murmuring from across the way. If those were some of The Dodo's men and they found me on this boat, this river crossing was definitely going to get a lot more exciting.

Allie seemed to be of the same mind. "They shouldn't see your face," she whispered, grabbing the back of my neck to pull my head down.

My forehead nearly pressed against hers, I shot her an incredulous look. "How is this better?"

"They're coming," she hissed. "Just shut up."

With Allie's warmth pressed against me, her breath on my cheek, the pit of my stomach stirred.

I wanted to get away. But at the same time...

I had to blink away drowsiness. I couldn't help but breathe in Allie's scent. Mostly engine grease and polished metal, but there was a faint flowery hint from—somewhere I couldn't pin down. I had to tamp down the urge to pull her even closer to ascertain *exactly where.*

The need to know was annoying me like the dickens. "Let me the hell go." My warning came out like a low rumble, tugged from a place deep inside. "Or else."

Her response was airy, self-assured. "Threaten me all you like. I know you can't hurt me right now." She cast a discreet backward glance again. "Shoot, they're not leaving. They're congregating in the bloody corridor."

I grumbled as I tried to push away but Allie yanked on my ear. "Mmff—" I almost couldn't stifle my groan of complaint but I happened to glance up the corridor, and spotting a lanky man with a beak-like mouth in a swanky red-striped coat, I jerked back against the wall hissing a curse under my breath. "That's him, The Dodo."

"Shoot." She dropped her gaze to think. "Maybe we should split up. You walk away. I'll try to distract them."

My dark gaze bore into her. "Nice try. I'm not letting you out of my sight."

"Oh, come on. I already know it's pointless to try to run away from you," she reminded me, trying to keep her voice as hushed as she could. Still frowning, she fidgeted in her stance. "They're going to see. Your face is too obvious at this angle."

Rolling my eyes in resignation, I braced my hands on her shoulders to spin us around so my back was to the corridor.

Allie gasped as she pressed up against the wall.

Propping up my arms to cage her face between them, I bent my head low to murmur close to her neck, beneath her ear. "Is this better then?"

Perhaps she noticed the relative ease with which I loomed over her; her one eyebrow quirked up in amusement. "I see this is not your first time tumbling along in dark corners. Is this why those women were chasing you? Did you seduce them all?" Her tone was still full of wonder as she studied my face.

Shifting slightly, I gave her the most deadpan look in my arsenal. "Girl, I have not even begun to do anything."

"So you just happen to be naturally irresistible to them?" she mused before stopping short. "Oh, I almost forgot. You used to be a bunny. The urge to copulate must be too strong to bear." Her shoulders began to shake in mirth.

Indignation rose in my chest again. "I am not an animal," I stated crisply.

Was she inferring that I was unable to control my own urges? And damn Chez for letting slip that very incriminating piece of information around Allie.

"Please," she chided in mocking. "I've been living underneath your loft for three weeks. You know all I've heard from your visiting lady friends? It always goes something like this—" Just then, Allie let out a low, pleasurable moan.

9

❦

Chapter Nine - Curious

My eyes nearly popped out at her noise. The vividness of her moan sent a bolt of desire straight through my core. To be fair, it was a decent mimicry of one of my most recent companions. Incensed, I grabbed her shoulder in alert and rolled her back flat against the wall once more. "Are you actually trying to get us caught?"

The Dodo and his men were walking down the hall, coming closer and closer to our darkened nook. Clever blocking was not going to disguise the fact of who I was. Much worse, if the animals caught wind of anything at all suspicious about Allie's nature, I could risk losing the *coeur*.

Dammit.

I racked my brain to think.

Across the corridor, I spotted a cleaner carrying a mop exiting a cabin he must have just finished cleaning. Eyes lighting up, I grabbed Allie's arm and pulled her across and into the door before it locked shut behind him.

Or at least I'd thought it was a door to a cabin.

"Ow!" Allie hissed as she slammed against a supply shelf.

I almost stumbled in the pitch dark. Ammonia and salts bathed the air around us in the cramped space—of the cleaning closet.

"Well, this is much better," Allie drawled. Feeling around for a light switch, she tugged on a little string and the dimmest bulb ever lit up the dank closet. Not exactly helpful.

I leveled a dark gaze at her. "Stop talking. And definitely stop moaning like that," I snapped. "Don't you know it's rude to eavesdrop on other people's intimate acts?"

She scoffed. "How could I not eavesdrop when all those women were so loud? To tell the truth, I'm a bit glad they haven't been coming around lately. I'm finally managing to get a decent night's sleep. I mean seriously, you guys would go at it for hours and hours and hours—"

I gritted my teeth. As proud as I was of my libido, hearing Allie refer to my sexual conquests with a certain banality was grating on my nerves.

"God only knows what the hell you were doing to those women all night long, makes it sound like they're being murdered—then again, you are an assassin, and a rabbit," she rambled on.

She was driving me crazy.

Without warning, I pushed her back against the closed door, grasping the nape of her neck, and leaned down.

"What the hell are you doing?" she gasped, pawing my face away. Those ridiculous glasses fell in the darkness.

My eyes flashed as I pressed my body against hers. I just wanted to shut her up. "I thought perhaps you wanted a proper demonstration." My gaze dropped to that annoying mouth. "The other day you asked me to kiss you."

She tilted her head back as far away from me as she could. "Right, perhaps if my life depended on it. Plus if you recall, I was seriously high the other day." Her eyes glittered in the dark. "Besides, I already told you I'm not seducible."

"That's what all those women said," I relayed confidently, stroking the side of her face with my thumb. "Before they fell under my spell and I carved their hearts out."

I had intended for my statement to be disarming, intimidating, but I was distracted by how smooth her cheek was. That flowery scent was close by again. I bent my head lower, closer, in an attempt to seek it out.

The sudden lack of protest from Allie made me stop short. She didn't try to push away either. Perhaps my declaration was a little more than disarming. When I looked into her face, her gaze was distracted off to one side in deep thought.

A shadow crossed her face. It was the vivid memory of the devastating slaughter back at Veridia. The heart in my chest gave a dull thump in the tense silence.

Allie swallowed hard. "Rabb...why do you do this for the Queen?"

I stopped short at her question. Her mouth was still a mere breath away from mine. "I have to. I'm bespelled to follow her commands."

"That's all?"

I pulled back an inch. "The Queen saved my life."

"Saved your life? How?" Curiosity filled her eyes, but there was also a certain measure of...pity.

I dropped my hands from her and straightened up. "I was cursed. My soul trapped in the form of a rabbit. I was about to die and the Queen saved me. We made a deal. She would restore my life, my human form, and in exchange, I would dedicate my immortal existence to serving her."

"By seducing women? By luring them to follow you and then stealing their hearts?"

"Yes. I lure them from their lives and they return...a little less."

"You said she extracts magic from them, the hearts. I bet if she stole your heart, she must have gotten so much power from it."

"I told you I no longer remember ever having had a heart. Even if I did, an immortal heart would be useless," I explained. "What makes Heartfire embers so magical is their limitations. It's the brief spark of power such that mortality can give, knowing that life is fleeting, that no matter how much you have, no matter how well you live, eventually you will lose everyone you love."

Her eyes seemed pinned to my mouth as I spoke. "But doesn't love last forever?"

This encounter seemed different from when I cornered her at my clock tower. This time, her aura seemed...curious, instead of laced with fear.

"Perhaps that's the trick." I shrugged. "How love can be fleeting and yet eternal." I cleared my throat after a moment. "But as I've mentioned, since I have neither a heart nor a plethora of loved ones, my Heartfire ember would have been useless."

Allie's gaze averted to one side again, as if to absorb my words to understand their full meaning.

I studied those hazel eyes in the dim light. It was beginning to fascinate me how well Allie kept her wits about her, managing to ask me thoughtful probing questions, all despite my close proximity. Such behavior was certainly unheard of.

Moving to one side, Allie pressed her ear to the door. "I think they might be gone." She turned the knob and cracked the door open to peek outside and see if the coast was clear before swinging it open more fully. But as soon as I stepped out behind her, there was a yell.

"Oi, you there!"

Halting, Allie cringed.

I stopped in mid-stride before turning to see two of The Dodo's men rounding the corner toward us.

The first mousy gentleman with a whiskery mustache stuck his little nose up in the air. "Were you just in that there closet eavesdropping on our private conversation?"

"N-No sir." Allie shook her head instantly. "We were just..."

I finished her sentence with a clear, authoritative tone, "—trying to sneak in a moment of pleasure. We couldn't be bothered to find our cabin."

Out of the corner of my eye, I saw Allie suck in her cheeks at my outrageous claim but she didn't say anything to the contrary.

"Maybe we ought to report you to The Dodo, hey Bill?" Mr. Mouse elbowed his colleague, the other one with an elongated lizard-like mouth.

Bill looked from Allie to me in turn, his eyes narrowed. "They are acting mighty suspicious."

I didn't want to waste any more time with these duds. I hooked my arm around Allie's neck to drag her away and she yelped out. "Hey—" I paused to think quickly. "Mary Ann, I think we'd better leave these gentlemen to their business and head to our cabin to continue our affairs."

Allie shot me a sideways glare. I was probably choking her. But her expression shifted into a sickeningly sweet smile as she gave me a playful shove away. "Oh, of course. I would be only so happy to. Come on, Steven."

I winced.

Steven?

Bill was craning his neck to peer at my face. "You know what, you look kind of familiar. Have we met before?"

Allie waved his claim away. "Oh, I'm sure a fine gentleman such as yourself has never met us lowly folk."

Turning his attention to her, Bill leered before reaching for her arm. "Is that one of them birds from upstairs? I haven't sampled this one yet. Let me see your pretty face, Miss—"

There was a sudden sting of displeasure in my chest. Eyebrows snapping together, I caught his hand to twist his arm behind him and slammed him face-first against the wall. My warning was a low growl in my throat, "Touch her and die."

"H-Hey, what are you doing?" His nasty colleague backed up in wide-eyed dread. "I-I'm gonna call the boss!" he yelled out as he scrambled away before his friend could even yelp.

It seemed The Dodo's dogs were all bark and no teeth.

"Let me go, you bastard." Bill struggled against my grasp.

"I'll make sure you pay for this. You and your little girl-friend too."

Allie heaved an exasperated sigh. "Jeez, let him go."

I rolled my eyes in resignation, but the moment I loosened my hold on Bill, he spun around, rearing back his arm to punch me in the face.

"You loathsome f—!"

It didn't take much to weave away to avoid his laughable aim. But before I knew what was happening, Allie moved in to deliver a swift knee between Bill's legs and he collapsed with a howl.

"Let's go," Allie urged, whirling around to run away.

I glanced at Bill, a crying heap on the floor as he clutched at his groin, and shrugged before following suit behind Allie as we ran up the stairs.

I couldn't help my remark. "Steven is a terrible name."

Somehow that made Allie laugh. "And Mary Ann is what? Your most favorite name in the whole entire world?" Her gaze sliding over my shoulder, her smile faded. "Oh, crapshoot."

The saloon behind us was quickly filling with an angry mob of more ruffians, headed directly for the stairwell.

For us.

Annoyed, I clicked my tongue. I *could* possibly fight them all. I glanced over at Allie, her eyes wide with overwhelm. There was no guarantee that I could protect her at the same time. Without my magic, it would be too risky.

I backed up. "Go, out the side door," I told her and followed suit as we ran down the narrow passageway along the side railing to head to the rear in an attempt to delay the inevitable fight.

When we reached the stern where the big paddle wheel furiously churned white water, I whirled back around.

Dead end.

Bracing my hands on the railing, I stopped to glance up the river. "We need to get off this boat now."

Allie checked up the way. "Are we close enough to the other side?"

"Please tell me you can swim," I prompted.

"I'm not the best but I can float."

"Good enough." I moved to help her up the side of the railing but she grabbed my arm.

"Wait." Her gaze was on the floor, her eyes narrowed as if ascertaining something. "The boat is moving too fast. It's not safe."

I glanced past her shoulder at the rushing mob of blood-thirsty thugs. "Well, it won't be safe on here for too long either."

Allie's gaze flicked out to the water and her eyes lit up. "I have an idea." She pointed across the water to a buoy marker. "There's a slight bend over there where the boat is likely to slow down. We just need to time it properly and then jump off the boat."

Reading her firm tone, I grumbled inwardly, but I knew there wasn't much choice.

"How much time until we reach the buoy?" I wanted to know.

Allie bit her lip. Her eyes darted around as she was seemingly trying to figure out something in her head and mumbling incoherently.

I narrowed my eyes. "Are you trying to calculate the

velocity of the steam boat against the drag of the river current based on our distance to the buoy?"

She gave me a look of ridicule. "No, that's crazy. I'm listening for the slowing down of the steam engine."

But the noise of the mob was getting louder too, footsteps clattering on the wooden deck, on the metal stairs, and even beneath us. They were going to surround us soon.

"Allie!" I prompted in urgency.

She waved me away with a screech, "Shush!"

The fastest pair of the thugs was about to come upon us. I groaned in exasperation as I surged forward to take them on. I blocked an onslaught of punches before whirling around to deliver each thug swift kicks in the face. But as they fell at my feet with a clatter, two more sets of thugs jumped down from the top level of the boat, landing right in front of me.

I clenched my teeth to shoot Allie another look. "Allie!"

Allie kept blinking then she flinched in a startle upon satisfaction of her assessment. She met my gaze. "NOW!"

Hurrying back, I hoisted Allie up the side of the railing so she could jump off.

Her gaze widened, spotting something over my shoulder. She tried to warn me, "Rabb!" but she had already fallen back into the water.

A sharp pain gouged deep in my shoulder. Yelling out a groan, I lurched over, easily tipping over the railing.

The roar of the mob turned faint as I dove headlong into the rushing cold water.

10

Chapter Ten - Beware Rainbows

"I hate this river." I spat as I hauled myself out, pulling the knife from my shoulder with a grunt. At some point during the swim, the hat and elastic Allie had insisted I put on had both washed away.

Almost disappearing through the mist, the steamboat sailed off and away down the river continuing on its cruise as though nothing had even happened.

Panting as she dragged herself onto the shore, Allie shot me an incredulous look. "What was your plan exactly? You thought you were going to fight all of them off? You shouldn't have attacked that one guy."

"Good thing you kicked him in the nuts. Save him that misery," I huffed, not understanding her concern. I may not have had my magic but I was certain I was still at least three times stronger than any of The Dodo's pathetic thugs.

"I had to do something," Allie pointed out. "You couldn't just go around breaking people's arms."

"I wasn't going to break his arm," I corrected. "I was going to kill him."

Allie groaned. "And what else, oh great and deadly assassin? You didn't want to torture him first?"

I shot her a look. "We didn't have time for torture."

"Oh, of course! How silly of me." She shook her head in disbelief. "This is just great." She wrung out her hands, her drenched outfit still dripping.

Clutching at my injured shoulder, I groaned at the sting. "For god's sake, help me," I rasped in annoyance as blood ran onto my clothes, diluted by the fresh river water. "Aren't you a doctor?" I gestured to her lab coat.

"Oh, hell." Allie threw her hands up. "I'm not that kind of doctor!"

Grunting again, I pressed my hand against my wound. We were still too close to the river for my magic to awaken. We were both soaking wet. I glanced distastefully down at myself. "We're going to need to get out of these wet clothes."

Allie made a big show of turning to give me an incredulous, wary look.

I knew exactly what she was thinking. "What?" I prompted again in exasperation. "I just meant so we don't catch a cold. How do you propose we get dry otherwise? By running around in circles?"

"For a moment there, I thought you were trying to pick up where we left off when we were—how did you say it?" She tapped her finger on her chin. "Trying to sneak in a moment of pleasure."

I sneered. "Do you think I'm still trying to seduce you, *Mary Ann*? I told you I don't have feelings like normal humans."

Allie still looked in disbelief. "Oh and what? Are you saying you were never attracted to those pretty women companions that visited you night after night after night for all your nocturnal activities?"

"I never had *feelings* for them. Attraction is different," I told her. "It just makes achieving release easier. But even that is not necessary." I dismissed her ridiculous tangent with a shake of my head and struggled to straighten up. "We need to get much further away from the river if I am to regain my magic."

She eyed my gait. "Are you sure you can walk? I think you lost a lot of blood."

I hissed at the sting in my shoulder. "Don't have much choice."

Allie's face still looked like she'd eaten lemons.

I rolled my eyes. "Wipe that look of pity off your face." I wanted to saunter away but with my first step, I already had to grunt in pain.

Allie caught my arm before I stumbled. "Jeez, Rabb. For a fearsome, daunting guy, how can you be such a big baby?"

The veins in my neck bulged in protest. I was the most goddamned powerful sorcerer on Wünder. Before Allie, things like this never happened to me on a daily basis. This was all her fault!

Of course, I couldn't choke the life out of her. I couldn't hold her head under the water and watch the bubbles slowly dissipate as she fought for breath. At the moment, I could barely keep my body upright.

I blew out all my pent-up frustration in a loud, aggravated, resigned sigh. And all I could do was make a face and mumble under my breath in my defense, "Am not."

As we went on, the sandy ground from the riverbank turned into more solid soil beneath our feet. Soon, we were on a distinctly well-trodden path in the middle of a rainforest.

Still supporting the crook of my arm, Allie glanced over her shoulder as we passed a wooden sign by the side of the path. "Why does that say 'Beware rainbows'?"

I gave her a flat look. "Rainbows are dangerous things. Don't you know anything?"

She tilted her head. "Why? What's so dangerous about rainbows?"

I sighed again to explain. "If you are unlucky enough to walk into a rainbow, you might reach its end where it may grant you the greatest wish of your heart in that moment."

"You're kidding. Like a treasure?" Allie gaped. "You're telling me there's really a treasure at the end of rainbows?"

"That's what I said." I groaned again. "It's pointless."

"It's brilliant!" Her eyes lit up like an epiphany. "Do you think if we found a rainbow, it could show me a portal to get back home?"

I stopped short. I hadn't considered that. I hadn't considered that we would encounter a rainbow either. If the rainbow did indeed show her a way home, my entire plan would fail. I needed to dissuade her from engaging the rainbow. Not that I really needed to try. In my experience, rainbows were atrocious things.

I cleared my throat. "Perhaps. But rainbows are tricky. Often it will interpret your wish in an unexpected way, or give you a mere one part of something even when you wished for a whole thing. They're highly unpredictable and very dangerous."

"Are you kidding me?" She dropped my arm to wander around as if on a hunt for it. "If it could give me a way to get out of this place? Worth a shot, I'd say." She walked backward, casting her gaze around the clearing. "So, where is this illustrious, magical rainbow that's supposed to be around here somewhere?"

I furrowed my eyebrows almost in mocking. "I thought you were a scientist? Don't you know you can't have a rainbow without—"

A crackle of thunder interrupted my sentence and a drizzle began to fall from the gray clouds that were rolling.

"Rain!" Allie exclaimed. Her face lit up with a childlike joy as she tilted her chin up to the sky. She closed her eyes for a moment as if to savor the sensation of the droplets falling on her face.

One corner of my mouth turned up ever so slightly.

Ignorance must indeed be bliss. Allie had absolutely no idea she was summoning one of the most treacherous things in all of Wünder. She even seemed...carefree, relaxed.

She smiled. "Mmm...That feels so good."

My mouth twitched. "Be careful. You're beginning to sound like those women again who keep me company at night."

Allie's laughter was as delicate as the rain. "I wasn't even trying before. Shall I do another one? Here." She let out an exaggerated moan—except she sounded like a cow about to be slaughtered.

I cringed. She sounded wholly ridiculous. But quite unexpectedly, I was unable to help letting out a short cough of amusement.

Allie's eyes widened larger than Chez's in abject surprise.

I supposed she didn't even know I could make that noise.

"Did you just…" She turned to face me. "That sound just now—was that actually laughter?"

There was an undeniable lightness in my chest. The prospect of finding a rainbow and potentially a way home must have triggered great joy in Allie. And it made me…laugh.

She continued to peer closely at my face. "Are you going to do it again?" she coaxed. "Come on, Rabb. Do you want to hear a joke? A limerick?" She cleared her throat. "There once was a man from Nantucket…" She paused in hesitation. "Something about a bucket that could suck it. I think he had a daughter named Nan. Who took the cash in the bucket—wait. Did he go down a well?" She stopped to think before starting again, "Wait, wait, wait. I think I have it." She waved her hand as if in ceremony. "There once was a man from Nantucket. Whose john was so long he could s—"

"Stop it." I shot her an absurd look, even though I was struggling to contain a smirk from the ridiculous look on her face. "Stop trying to make me laugh."

Allie was finding the situation entirely too amusing. Her melodious laughter rang in the air. "I wonder if your rainbows have the same colors as the ones I know. Red, yellow, orange…" She cast me a glance. "What's your favorite color?"

I glared at her again. "Black."

She pursed her lips. "That's not a color."

"Of course it is."

Allie shook her head. "Well, no. Technically, black is the absence of all color. Which is interesting because it's also the presence of all the colors, I suppose…"

A streak of sunlight broke through the lingering clouds above us and an arch of vibrant hues emerged. The rainbow glistened in the air, an ethereal bridge connecting the ground to the skies. The phenomenon put a halt to her rambling.

Allie's breath caught in her throat. "There it is!" Running to the bow, she screeched to a stop and put her foot on the edge that touched the ground to test its stability. Her toe bounced on the multi-colored lip before the first step. "Huh. Springy."

Frowning, I put my hand up. "Be careful."

She stepped forward, following the trail of patterned colors, in no way apprehensive. I could feel her eagerness to see the end, to see the treasure. The hope in her heart that she should find a way home was making her heart thump again.

I followed behind her on cautious alert.

I had heard of people surviving rainbows before so it wasn't entirely impossible. But it was better to be safe.

The haze of the rainbow was masking the dimness of the forest. The path to the end was now lined with fluffy white clouds, adorned with sparkles, daytime stars, and bright light.

Allie was looking around in marvel. "Wow! Would you look at all these things?"

I squinted at the appearance of objects lining the rainbow lane. Wooden chests of gold coins and jewels, a selection of glittering dresses and shoes, shelves full of books, and a wide array of delectable food flanked us.

I pursed my lips. "Don't touch anything. That is the test of the rainbow. If you really want the thing you seek, the one treasure at the end, you must resist being tempted by anything else."

Allie raised her hand to shield her eyes from the bright light as we neared the end. "I can't tell what it is. It doesn't look like a portal or a doorway. It's too small. Is that..."

I narrowed my eyes, already in incredulous suspicion at the strange object hovering at the end of the lane. It was a small package, rolls of pristine white bandages, little jars of ointment, and brown bottles of medicine. "What the hell is that? Is that a...?"

Allie's mouth had dropped open like she couldn't believe it either.

No way.

The rainbow was gifting Allie a healing burlap.

Her hazel eyes met mine before her gaze drifted down to my injured shoulder. "Did *you* ask for this?"

"Hey, you're the one who stepped on the rainbow first," I reminded her. "Did *you* ask for that?" I couldn't help the mocking in my tone.

She threw her hands up in dismay. "Well, this is so wrong! There's no way I wished for this. There has to be some kind of mistake."

I tilted my head to regard her with a mocking look. "Are you sure? The deepest wish of your heart isn't to heal my shoulder and coddle me until I get better? You said I couldn't but perhaps I already have succeeded in seducing you."

She rolled her eyes. "You're ridiculous. That's preposterous. And anything is better than that stupid thing." Turning on her heels, her eyes caught something by the side of the path. "Oh my god, look! It's a laser micro-scalpel—and that—that's an electron microscope. I've wanted one for ages!"

Allie's hand reached out to the microscope as if in slow motion.

Eyes widening, my stomach hollowed. "Allie—NO!"

The moment her fingertip touched the eyepiece, a gust of wind rushed past as a tangle of sinewy, twisting vines shot out from behind us.

Allie's yelp of surprise was cut short as tendrils coming from the rainbow's end, moving with a deceptive speed, reached out to ensnare her body, entwining around her with a serpentine agility.

The rest of the rainbow shrugged me off its shimmering path and I staggered back to the forest floor.

"Ah, hell—" Cursing out loud, I wrung my arms out to cast a repellent spell but my powers still had not returned. *Damn that river!* Straightening up, I assessed the vicious vines in concern. "Allie!"

"Ah, dammit!" Allie's face twisted in the effort as she tried to tug at the leafy cords wrapped around her arms. "It's fine!" she called out to dismiss. "It's just a plant. I can get myself out."

The tangle of vines rose higher from the ground with Allie in its grasp, her legs dangling beneath her, suspended nearly as high as some of the trees around us. Then this bramble of vines, slowly but surely, began to crawl along the forest floor.

I stepped back, preparing to get some momentum to take

a run at the vines—but instead, I collapsed to one knee. I clutched at my throat as it threatened to close up. I shot the menacing plant a dark glare.

With an almost sentient malevolence, the unrelenting grip of the leafy vines around Allie was constricting tighter in a coil. She was starting to suffocate.

The rainbow was showing its true colors. It was a beast that lured its prey with the sweetest of honeys before it devoured them, a predatory trap for those with flights of fancy. Its shadowy monstrous form swelled from the ground with Allie still in its python grip.

She choked out a cry and I groaned at the same time as the monster squeezed harder.

It was like I was in a vise. Large red welts forming on my arms began to sting like hell.

Allie cried out again.

I hissed as I tried to keep up. My eyes could only widen as the menacing vines began to sprout a nightmare of thorns all over. Telltale bleeding cuts were forming on my arms. If this went on, I would lose my strength too.

Allie's next whine was fainter. The mere sound tore at my insides.

Almost with a shout of outrage, I forced my body straight, darting back to bound off of a nearby tree so I could pounce on the rainbow monster's elevated tangle of vines.

Coming to reach Allie, I clawed on the rough tendrils constricted around her even as the monster rumbled on, possibly looking for somewhere to quietly digest its meal.

Allie's eyelids were drooping. She was about to lose consciousness. I didn't have much time.

A surge of energy shot through my body as my magic reawakened. I blinked in realization. The monster must have finally moved us far enough away from the river.

With my renewed strength, I tore at the vines again. This time, they disintegrated under my hands. I scooped Allie up in my arms and shot off to fly us away.

But the darkness of the monster's insides had taken over the bright colors surrounding us. It was sucking us in and was going to swallow us whole. No matter how fast I flew us upward, we couldn't seem to escape its pitch-dark clutches. I could barely even tell if we were flying out or getting sucked in deeper.

Dammit!

Slowly regaining consciousness, Allie mumbled a complaint in my arms.

"I told you rainbows were dangerous!" I couldn't resist pointing out.

Her face was still sour but as she got her bearings back, her grip around my neck tightened. "Oh, come on. I thought you were the most powerful sorcerer in Wünder?"

"Sorcerers are one thing. Beasts are another," I pointed out, struggling to keep up our pace.

The wind whipping past her face, her eyelids seemed to droop again. She still seemed halfway lucid. "Kill it. Kill it with fire."

"What?"

Fire magic was a tricky thing to conjure, perhaps the trickiest. Wary of the considerable drain on my powers, I would likely only have one shot at the beast. It was too big for me to stab with my dagger.

"I have a theory," Allie proposed.

I barely stifled the urge to groan. *Oh, here we go again.*

"No, listen, it only makes sense. Rainbows are light reflected in water droplets. Subjected to extreme heat, if those drops were to evaporate, there would be nothing for light to pass through, so—"

Screw it. I didn't bother waiting for her to finish. I had to try something.

Gritting my teeth, I waved my hand to conjure a fire to repel the beast. A bright orange flame from my hand grew larger and larger until it enveloped Allie and me. I squinted at my hand. This fire was somehow more intense than I'd ever conjured before.

Not stopping to analyze my surprise, I took a deep breath and flicked my wrist to disperse my fire at the beast.

The monster's roar was loud in my ears. The dark gooey plasma around us wobbled and shook as my fire spread across its entire form. Heat seared my face but I tucked Allie's head in my chest as I flew us up faster and faster, until soon, I could see the light at the end of the whorl of burning beast, like a tunnel.

Shooting out of the rainbow's maw, we arrived back in the forest. I grasped the nearest tree to catch us, its trunk nearly swinging at the force. With a precarious grip on the branch we'd landed on, I glanced back in time to see the dark beast explode into a million shimmery pieces with a devastating gust of wind that raged across the forest. The intensity of the explosion gouged a blackened impact crater on the ground.

The rainbow was completely obliterated.

Allie peeked out, her eyes still wide as she gazed at all the fallen trees around us. "Whoa. Did you just...?"

For once, I was at a loss.

I hadn't meant to do that. I didn't even know destroying rainbows was possible. Then again, I'd never had to fight a rainbow before. I would've never had cause to do so before and they weren't that prevalent on my side of the river.

But surprise was secondary to the load of relief in my chest and then—fury. I glared at Allie in disapproval. "And just what in the hell were you trying to do?"

"I-I'm sorry."

I set Allie down on the semi-wobbly thick branch beside mine. "I honestly can't tell if you're really brave...or just really dumb."

Rubbing her arms, she wrinkled her nose. "I was curious."

I groaned again. If I had a Heartfire ember for every time Allie said that. "Haven't you heard of that saying, like what happens with cats and curiosity?" I ran my hand over my face in frustration. "You should ask Chez. More than a couple of his lives were lost thanks to curiosity."

"I said I was sorry." Allie pouted as she adjusted her clothes.

A cat's head popped up right by my shoulder among the leaves.

Allie almost jumped back into my arms in her startle.

"Someone mention my name?" Chez grinned as the rest of his fuzzy purple body slowly followed to appear.

Half in relief, Allie clutched at her chest. "Chez! How did you get here?"

"I'm a Cheshire cat. I can go anywhere I want." He stood

on his hind legs and mocked a formal bow. "Besides, I'm here to escort you to the Duchess's humble abode."

Scooping Allie back up, I flew us back to the ground and set her down on the grass.

Teetering slightly on her feet, she winced. Her white coat had bleeding punctures from the thorny vines. I was sure she had the same red welts I did. It was lucky we managed to escape before the beast could injure her more seriously.

Chez looked from her to me with a shake of his head. "Jeez, you guys look horrible. Allie, are you sure you're okay?"

She was nursing her arm with one hand. She shook her head dismissively but her nose was still wrinkled. "It stings a little but I'll be okay. I think Rabb got me out in time."

The purple cat popped up ahead of us on the grassy path. He craned his neck back to muse, "Hey Rabb, saw what you did just then with that rainbow monster. That was pretty impressive."

"Of course it was." I dismissed him, but as soon as I strode after him, I winced at the throbbing pain myself. Now I had a stab wound in my shoulder *and* bleeding thorny cuts all over. I hissed under my breath as I tried to conjure a healing spell to no avail.

Juuust great...

My magic was sapped. I couldn't heal myself.

Hobbling along, Allie frowned as she looked me up and down. "You know, for a bad guy, you have an incredibly incorrigible hero complex." She shook her head in disapproval. "You were already hurt and you jumped in like that. You probably tapped out your mystical core all over again, didn't you?"

Whirling around, I growled in her face. "I had to! How the hell else would I keep you safe?"

She winced, leaning away, and let out an exasperated sigh. "You keep saying that. Is my life that important to you?"

Leveling my gaze with hers, I was sure my tone was as grave as anything. "I *told* you it's as important as my own life."

Blinking, Allie studied my eyes for a silent moment. It was as though, despite my having told her the same thing on multiple occasions, it had only finally sunk in. She pursed her lips after a pause. "Well then, you'd better take better care of yourself. Or how else are you going to have enough strength to step in to save me again next time?"

Flinching in annoyance, I fumed. "Next time?"

Allie couldn't help bursting out with laughter, even as she had to stop short to clutch at her sore torso. "Oh, ow—I'm just kidding." She shook her head again. "You're such a downer."

Chez chuckled to himself as he led the way down the lane. "Come along then. When we get to the Duchess's, you'll both be set right."

Chapter Eleven - Meet the Duchess

I hadn't been to the Duchess's house for decades.

I supposed for someone seeing it for the first time, the large country estate, with its ornate wrought-iron balconies wrapped around the structure, held a certain architectural charm. Even if the sprawling lush gardens were noticeably overgrown, the trees moss-draped, the front lawn unkempt. The property was set amidst a wetland of willow trees with trailing tendrils and branches dangling to touch the water's tranquil surface.

Chez sashayed down the grass-covered path that led to the porch.

The throbbing from my injuries had subsided somewhat. I glanced over at Allie walking partway behind me. "The Duchess will not like you."

She didn't seem perturbed by this. "Were you lovers?" she asked, adjusting the bandanna we had haphazardly bound around her arm for a particularly deep gash. It was as much as I could do after having even failed to retrieve the healing burlap from the rainbow.

"Yes," I replied without hesitation.

As the case was with anyone else *except* Allie, the Duchess was not immune to my charms. She had no substantial Heartfire ember of her own for me to steal. Our dalliances had always been brief and casual. Not to mention quite a long, long time ago.

Back then, trips across the River of Tears had been relatively painless. The Duchess was held to a very high regard on this side, as well as with The Dodo's men. And with her on my arm, nobody had ever dared to cross my path.

But again, that was a long, long time ago.

I'd had to stop seeing the Duchess since she discovered that I was the only immortal being on Wünder who could fulfill her one, burning desire.

"So what is it? You think she'll be jealous of me?" Allie asked, even as she inspected her damp clothes with a look of distaste.

"Probably." I shrugged. "But don't go getting your head any bigger, thinking you're special. She's jealous of all women. She can barely leave this place nowadays."

The potted string beans hanging above the porch swung in the warm breeze, squeaking a crooning song:

and the slithy toves
did gyre and gimble in the wabe:
all mimsy were the borogoves...

Chez leaped up the three steps and slipped through the cat door.

With my uninjured arm, I pulled the French doors open and gestured my hand for Allie to walk through and into the foyer. I grunted under my breath as the smallest strain pulled at my wounds anyway but it wasn't like I was new to a little pain and suffering. The door sighed at my gallantry but I merely rolled my eyes.

As soon as Allie stepped in, something above us caught her gaze and she jumped in alarm. "Oh my goodness!"

The Duchess, a petite, stocky woman in her puffy-sleeved, frilly dress with voluminous layers, was, at that moment, atop an awkward ladder attaching the end of a lead of rope around her neck, whilst the other end was firmly tied around the large extravagant crystal chandelier installed upon the ceiling.

Allie ran to her aid. "Madame!" she cried out. "Are you quite alright?" Pacing beneath the Duchess, she wrung her hands out in a fluster. "Rabb! Help her! Do something!"

I stuck my hands in my pockets and simply walked past the scene. "Leave her be."

"What?" Allie's eyes were wide with outrage. "How can you even say that?"

Navigating toward the small bar where liquor had been set out in crystal decanters on little trays, I let out a sigh as I poured myself a drink. "Allie," I began, matter-of-factly. "She's immortal."

Chez hopped up to the bar beside me. "Is the Duchess on the chandelier again?" he prompted, sounding in no way concerned either as he pawed at a fuzzy ball of yarn.

Allie tried to process the information, looking from Chez

and back to me, then glancing back up at the frumpy form of the Duchess who had stalled whilst stepping off the precarious ladder.

The Duchess blew the blonde hair out of her eyes, her face crumpling up in complaint. "Dammit, Rabb. I am making it so easy for you. After all these years, will you not please kill me already?"

I was intimately familiar with her aggravated tone. It was combined with haggardness, an exhaustion that could only come from having had to do the same job all these years and centuries. And unfortunately for the Duchess, her only escape was the sweet release of death only an assassin's hand could deliver.

Allie's eyes were still round and wide. For a mortal, I supposed it was unheard of for someone to wish for death so ardently.

"You'll have to forgive the Duchess," Chez mewled to appease Allie. "She is given to histrionics."

Letting out another disgruntled half-groan, half-sigh, the Duchess gave a wave of her hand, and with a pop, she appeared standing before me at the bar. Prim and proper, she adjusted the frills of her dress, and the curls of her blonde hair, her question directed at me. "And to what shall I attribute the honor of your presence here in my humble abode?" She met my even gaze with a raised eyebrow. "After so many unanswered invitations?"

My gaze slid over to Allie. "Chez," I called out. "Why don't you take Allie on a tour of the grounds first? I'm sure she'd love it."

Allie jumped in her stance. "Oh, no, I'm sure I'd rather stay."

"But I'm sure you'd love to go," I insisted, giving her a narrow-eyed look. "Go. Love it."

Allie gave me an indignant look.

With an almost mock ridicule, I met her gaze evenly. Did she think she had any more cards to play? If she threw a fit right then, I would have the Duchess toss her in the cellar.

Chez blinked at me, then Allie, then me again. "Right. Hey Allie," he coaxed, leaping off the bar and walking toward the door. "Let's leave these two long-separated love birds to catch up first. For sure, the sight of them canoodling together is not something you'll want filling in those memories."

That brought a look of distaste on Allie's face.

"You'll come back right in time for supper, my darlings." The Duchess waved them away, beaming a pleased smile. "Oh, and if you spot my little pet running around the grounds, would you be a dear and grab it for me?"

Allie had that curious look on her face again. "What sort of pet do you have?"

"Oh, it might look like a pig. Or a baby."

Allie's eyebrows shot up at the oddity. "Oh. Right. Of course. Sure, that makes sense."

I couldn't help a scoff at the critical look on her face. "Just because it doesn't make sense to you doesn't mean it doesn't make sense at all."

Sticking her tongue out at me, Allie butchered an awful curtsy before turning on her heel to leave.

I sighed. I couldn't quite figure out why Allie's criticisms of Wünder as being nonsense always struck me as personally offensive but they did.

"Are you going to start bringing your women across the river now?" The Duchess's arm slinked around mine. "Or did you have something special in mind on this occasion?" Her eyes twinkled as she spoke. "You know I've been longing for your company."

"The river makes it tricky to visit, as you well know." I set my glass down.

Turning to face me, the Duchess walked her fingers up my chest as she leaned in, overwhelming me with her powdery dogwood scent. "Your clothes are all wet."

I pushed her away.

Staggering back, she pouted. "You're no fun anymore, Rabb."

"You'll have to excuse me then. It's certainly no fun being with someone who tries to get me to kill them. I would never have cause to kill you as the Queen would never command it."

"The Queen can shove it," she bit out. "Just because she holds our leash doesn't mean we can't do what we want."

I didn't respond. Had the Queen commanded me to end the Duchess's life, I wouldn't have hesitated. But the Duchess's work was integral to keeping the Queen in power. Nobody else in Wünder was ever able to harm her. Except maybe me.

She let out another labored sigh. "Well then, why don't we just cut to the chase and you tell me why you are here."

Wholly unaccustomed to what I was about to say, I pursed my lips in hesitation first. "I...need your help." Even saying the wretched words brought a stitch to my chest.

But the Duchess merely let out an airy laugh. She beckoned

me over. "Come. Let's see what Cook has prepared for us today."

The Duchess led me to the conservatory where the floor-to-ceiling glass windows let in the late afternoon light, bathing the plants and flowers around the tea table setup. The flowers in their pots were jumping around and pushing the other plants out of their way to be in direct sunlight.

"Quiet!" The Duchess snapped her fingers and the flower pots all clanked still where they stood. Walking along, she rubbed her hands together. "Ooh, can you smell that? Cook has baked some lovely peppered bread."

I peered out the side of the glass house. I couldn't see where Chez had taken Allie.

The Duchess noticed my attention veering away. "I'm sure they'll be back shortly. Please." She gestured to the spread of food before us. "Help yourself." Situating herself upon a tall white padded armchair, she shrugged. "And pray tell, what sort of help do you need from me that warrants all this fuss?"

Picking up a plate, I met her gaze evenly. "This girl has lost her memories. Without them, I cannot ignite her Heartfire ember."

"Ah." She sighed. "Ironhaven. I remember such a case."

"And?" I prompted eagerly. "Did the lady retrieve her memories when the Queen captured her heart?"

The Duchess paused for a beat. "Yes. As you perhaps already know, the magic of Heartfire embers is amplified by the connections people have made through their lives, their collections of loved ones, their shared memories. The Heartlamp unlocks all this power."

I nodded. "Yes, but can you tell me why some victims remain as ghosts and yet some die right away?"

"Oh, that depends on the Heartfire ember," the Duchess explained. "The more powerful the magic it contains, the less there is left over."

Perfect.

A little shiver of triumph shot through my body, I almost couldn't contain it.

My plan was going to work.

Almost spurred on, I picked out more food to load my plate. "Excellent. Then all I really need is a Heartlamp to contain her heart and get Allie's memories back, thus igniting her Heartfire ember."

Muted, the Duchess just nodded. "Tis true."

I moved along the platters of salty seafood, cured cuts of meat, and blocks of cheese.

Maybe Allie was fascinated by whatever sights Chez was showing her outside at the moment, but I was feeling a bit giddy at the prospect of acquiring the power of that *coeur.* Once I extracted that legendary mystical Heartfire ember power, I should be able to reenergize my clock tower and halt the countdown on my existence.

"Rabb?" The Duchess's call broke into my train of thought.

"What?" I blinked at her.

Her forehead was creased as she noticed what I was doing. "Why are you...sorting the food?"

I glanced down at the plate where I had quite noticeably pushed some mushy red fruit to one side as though afraid it would contaminate the rest of my selections. "Allie doesn't like tomatoes."

The Duchess's eyebrows shot up. "Really? How do you know that?"

Nonchalantly, I explained, "She always picks them out. Her food trays have always come back with them left over and when we were on the boat—"

Her mouth was slightly ajar in wonder.

Stopping, I clenched my jaw. "What?" I asked again, tersely this time.

She looked away. "Nothing," she dismissed. "I'm just...surprised you're doing that for her. Surprised you even noticed."

I froze.

Tilting her head, the Duchess gave me an amused look. "Did you only realize that yourself just now?"

My skin prickled. I dropped the fork I was holding and set the plate back down. "It doesn't mean anything."

I stepped back in dismay. My stomach stirred in unease. *That godforsaken woman,* I gritted my teeth almost in vindication. I was this close to being rid of her completely, and I would only be so glad.

"Oh Rabb, would you be a dear and hand me that knife?"

Still distracted, I moved to pick up the utensil. When I spun around, the Duchess was in mid-jump to throw herself at me in an attempt to impale herself on the knife.

I wove away just in time. "Seriously, Duchess." I shook my head at her with a dark glare.

The Duchess's shoes squeaked on the floor as she skidded to a stop—quite unharmed. Throwing up her hands, she blew out an aggravated breath through her pursed lips. "Fine! I give! You won't even give me the courtesy of ending my tedious life. What else have I got to do?" She marched right around the table to slump back in her padded throne.

Fidgeting in my stance, I craned my neck to check on Allie and Chez out the windows again. "Listen," I started, lowering my voice. "I am trying to get this girl to willingly deposit her heart in a Heartlamp, so I would appreciate it if you don't tell her what happens afterward. I told her I would help her go back home if she gave me her Heartfire ember."

The Duchess broke a conspiratorial smile. "My dear Rabb, you are as ruthless as ever." She put a finger to her lips. "Not a peep from me."

12

Chapter Twelve - Heartlamp

Strains of laughter at the doorway drew my attention as Allie and Chez walked through. I couldn't help but note how relaxed Allie was around Chez. The two of them looked like jolly old friends coming back from an adventure.

My eyebrows furrowed in displeasure. "What took you so long? I said to tour the grounds, not engage in some prolonged bonding activity."

Allie gave me a suffering look.

"Oh, we found your broken hydraulic sprinkler system," Chez started.

The Duchess put a hand to her mouth. "I forgot to mention. I hope you didn't hurt yourself. Those rusty taps and hoses are tangled up all over the place, sunken holes everywhere."

Chez's eyes lit up. "Oh, Allie fixed it."

The Duchess blinked. "What?"

My gaze slid over to Allie.

Allie shrugged. "The gears were just all mucked up from the humidity and I tightened some of the fittings. It should be running right as rain once again, green up all that nice grass you have."

At her offhand, self-assured response, the Duchess's eyes narrowed for a moment. Her thin red lips curved into a pleased, somewhat devious smile. "Hmm..." Her gaze went up and down Allie's figure as if seeing her for the first time. "You look like a drowned kitten, my dear." She snapped her fingers. "Dry clothes for everyone."

I jerked in my stance as, with a poof of sparkling mist, even my shirt and pants were dry and clean.

Allie's shirt was pristine once again, her lab coat freshly pressed, not a stain in sight. She gave the Duchess a pleased smile. "Thank you, Madame Duchess."

The Duchess gave her a magnanimous smile. "Shall we sit down to supper?"

With great enthusiasm, Allie plonked herself into a chair. Chez hopped to curl up on a little table beside the Duchess's chair with a little saucer of green soup set out on it.

"This looks wonderful." Allie served herself a bowl of the same green soup.

The Duchess's smile didn't waver. "We've got some lovely mock turtle soup today. Made from fresh mock turtles."

At that notion, Allie tilted her head and couldn't help her remark, "Fascinating." She dipped the spoon in the soup and let it drip back into the bowl a few times, watching it closely as though studying its consistency, before she tasted a mouthful with no apprehension whatsoever.

"How is it, dear?" the Duchess prompted.

Allie pursed her lips. I supposed she figured honesty was going to be the best tack. "It tastes like waffles." Then she paused as though not willing to give offense. "Tasty though."

Standing by the liquor trolley, I rolled my eyes and poured myself another drink.

Chez was licking his own lips. "Too much pepper."

Allie's smile widened with amusement. Her gaze fell on the plate nearest to me, the one with the tomatoes sorted out. "Are you eating that?"

"No." I pushed the plate away. "Look, can we finish up this meal so we can get to business? The Duchess will need some time to craft you a Heartlamp and then you should get your memories back."

The Duchess's mouth dropped open in mild surprise. "Oh, I'm sorry, Rabb. I think you misunderstood. I'm afraid I actually won't be able to do that."

"What?" Frowning in displeasure, I leaned against the table. "Is this because I won't give you what you want? Look, Duchess, I already told you. Without the Queen's command, I cannot—"

"Ah, but that is precisely the problem." The Duchess put her hand up. "I do have some Heartlamp pieces crafted and ready. But without one last ingredient which only the Queen can provide, my lamps will just be regular lamps. They won't hold even the faintest of Heartfire embers."

"What?" I stopped, stunned in almost outraged disbelief.

I met Allie's gaze. I'd half-expected her to be just as outraged but her forehead was merely creased in concern.

Checking my fury, I turned to glare at Chez. "You didn't tell me it was pointless to come here without the missing ingredient from the Queen."

Chez merely licked his paws. "What? I don't know everything." He winked at Allie then disappeared into thin air.

"So this whole trip was a waste." Impatient, I whirled around and paced across the floor. "Why did we even bother coming all this way?"

The Duchess lamented with a heavy sigh. "I wanted to see my Rabb one last time before I died."

"For the last time, Duchess, you're not going to die." I had to roll my eyes. "You want to know why? Because I'm not gonna kill you. No matter how much you beg."

"Wait." Allie was deep in thought, gears in her mind spinning. I could practically see the steam almost coming out of her ears. "So what you're saying is we need something from the Queen to make this Heartlamp work its magic?"

"Yes." The Duchess nodded.

Allie pointed between the Duchess and me. "And neither of you have enough magic mumbo jumbo to make it work on your own?"

"Tis true." The Duchess nodded again. "Short of dropping in on the castle and stealing the essence of hearts, there's no other way to activate a Heartlamp."

Allie's eyes narrowed in that way and I knew she was scheming something once again. "Well, why don't we? Go and steal this...*essence*, I mean." She shrugged. "The Queen steals people's hearts. She should get a dose of her own medicine."

"Why?" the Duchess echoed in mocking. "Because my dear the Queen would cut off your head sooner than you could hopscotch away. She is the most powerful being in Wünder."

Allie shot me a look. "More powerful than Rabb?"

There was an undefined twinge in my chest at her words, which if I dared overthink felt gratifyingly like pride.

"I thought he was the most powerful sorcerer in Wünder?"

Quashing the burgeoning warmth in my chest, I dropped my gaze. I was already aware the whole point was moot.

"The Queen's powers have no match," the Duchess stated ruefully. "Our magic, Rabb's and mine...could never be used against her."

"She's not wrong." A telltale silhouette of a yellow grin hovered in mid-air above Allie's shoulder, close to her face— perhaps a little too close.

Allie nearly jumped out of her skin. "Cripe!" She clutched her hand to her chest. "Chez! Can you please stop randomly appearing out of nowhere like that? You scared the brain cells out of me!"

Chez plopped onto the table with another grin. "Sorry."

Blowing out a breath, Allie put a finger on her chin. "So, okay...if this Heartlamp is built like a regular lamp, do we need the Duchess to build it or could we possibly take the pieces away and assemble it later?"

"A fair question." The Duchess gave Allie a scrutinizing look. "She looks handy with tools. I bet you can figure out how to make it yourself. Can't you, strange girl?"

"I can build anything," Allie declared. "So we know what it is though? This item we need from the Queen? Perhaps it's possible to acquire it somewhere else?"

The Duchess shook her head. "I am afraid, my dear, this is something unique to the Queen. There will be no other way to produce it without her hand."

"Nuts," Allie mumbled.

The Duchess's eyes lit up. "Unless perhaps you could try summoning a rainbow?"

I gave the Duchess a deadpan look. "Already fought a rainbow on the way here. I don't think we want to risk another encounter with that type of beast."

A look of surprise crossed the Duchess's face. "You didn't get what you desired from the rainbow?"

Allie cringed. "The rainbow had a pretty odd interpretation of what I desired."

A corner of my mouth turned up against my will. "Allie keeps insisting that she doesn't care about my well-being whilst managing to conjure a healing burlap for my injuries from the rainbow beast."

Shaking her head, Allie hissed. "You're still ridiculous."

The Duchess gaped at Allie, her eyes widening even more than before, as though something new had struck her. Naturally, it hadn't occurred to her that Allie would be any different. "Wait a minute. Are you..." She pointed a manicured finger at Allie but then slid her gaze over to me. "She's...*not* enamored by you?"

I cleared my throat but Allie answered before I could.

"No, *she* is not," Allie confirmed, her tone pointed. "But you should have seen these women on this boat," she went on with a mocking chuckle. "And all these other women he brings home at night. Have they never even seen a man before," she scoffed, "carrying on as though Rabb was the only remotely attractive one around?"

But the Duchess nodded. "Ah, 'tis true! It's his gift. And his curse. Rabb has stolen the hearts of many a female here in Wünder. There isn't a woman around that once Rabb sets his eyes upon, he cannot make fall in love with him, bend to his will, and make his own. Mind, body, heart, and soul. And once they are under his spell, it's that much easier to extract their mystical hearts and deliver to the Queen."

"Whaaaat?" Allie whined in a high-pitched tone. "That's ridiculous. You're saying he can make anyone fall in love with him?"

I flashed her a self-assured I-told-you-so smirk. "One look and they are mine."

Allie pointed at herself. "Except me?"

I huffed. "You are not an exception. I told you. You are already mine. Your life belongs to me."

"Nooo." Still in incredulous disbelief, Allie's nose was scrunched up, her fingers spread in question. "That is just— come on, *all of them*? I mean, what do they even see in him?"

The Duchess looked perplexed. "He's...gorgeous and pow- erful." Her expression overwhelmed with concern. "Oh dear, I think perhaps this girl is blind. She must be suffering from a malady worse than memory loss." Leaning forward, she waved her hands in Allie's face. "Her perception seems to be askew."

Weaving back, Allie folded her arms across her chest. "There is nothing wrong with my perception. I just...don't understand." She seemed to ruminate on it further. "Though I suppose the evidence does seem to support this. It's a wonder

Wünder isn't crawling with all your fluffy, little bunny babies given your rather frequent mating habits."

Hissing in annoyance, I gritted my teeth. "Shut up," I snapped before glaring at Chez again. "Dammit Chez. Did you really have to tell Allie about that?"

"I'm sorry." Chez snickered, looking in no way apologetic.

"Oh darling, does she know your animal form?" The Duchess looked amused.

"Chez told me." Allie's eager eyes turned to her. "Have you seen it?"

The Duchess nodded. "Oh, yes, it was quite cute."

The three of them laughed.

My glare as dark as I could make it, I merely shook my head. I didn't want to give them the satisfaction of blowing up. "Yes, let's just all have a laugh, shall we?" I drawled, my tone dripping with sarcasm. "And after this highly productive visit, we now have the problem of how to get back to our side of the river."

Stopping short, Allie made a face. "Oh right, we probably can't go back on the *Caucus*."

Chez's forehead was creased. "What sort of trouble did you cause on the boat this time? Did you get caught fooling around under the roulette tables again?"

"Doesn't matter," I dismissed curtly. "Either way, I am not getting back on that river so we'll have to find some other way."

"Ah! I know of a tree hollow," the Duchess spoke up. "'Tis the only one of its kind which you can use to cross the River of Tears."

Allie's eyes lit up. "Really?"

"Yes. However, there is only one way to get to it." The Duchess's tone was already wary.

My face fell. "No."

Allie looked from her to me. "What?"

"It's on the Hatter's property," the Duchess relayed with a helpless shrug. "And he's...not all there." She gestured a loopy motion with her hand, screwing up her face on purpose.

That made Chez roll over in stitches.

I hissed in displeasure. This trip was just getting better and better.

Even though the Hatter was technically a man, in my opinion, he was worse than the Jabberwocky and the rainbow beast combined.

"Perhaps he can still be reasoned with?" Allie proposed.

"Perhaps." The Duchess gave a wave. "Regardless, I think you ought to rest here a while before you continue on your journey. The overnight tides will be coming soon." She raised one hand to summon servants to lead us to our rooms.

"I'd like to stay and have a chat if you don't mind." Allie gave the Duchess an imploring nod.

"Excellent." The Duchess's eyes lit up. "More tea, please." She gave another wave to a butler standing by.

I sighed. I was absolutely not here on a social visit. Shrugging, I moved to take my leave and headed upstairs. "Suit yourselves."

13

Chapter Thirteen - Curiouser

After having washed up from supper, instead of resting, I stalked out of my quarters once again.

I couldn't sit still. My mind was too busy. Despite it being unlikely that we were in any danger, I was impatient for my magic to renew. I disliked feeling this powerless.

I was relieved the tinkling of teacups and general merriment from downstairs had already dissipated.

Chez was in a hammock hung along the upstairs balcony with his ball of yarn. He looked up as I walked past. "The Duchess has retired for the evening,"

"I didn't ask." Wrinkling my nose, I fussed with the itching on my shoulder wound. With my magic strained, I hadn't bothered to tend to it at all.

Flopping around on his belly, Chez watched me with big,

violet eyes. "Curious," he started. "Back there, at the rainbow? What was that? When Allie got hurt, you…"

I dropped my gaze. "I got hurt too."

Chez's eyes seemed to widen at the enormity of the conclusion my statement implied. "You mean if you hadn't saved her just then—"

"She would be dead," I said flatly. "Meaning, *I* would be dead. That woman will quite literally be the death of me."

Chez shook his head. "Sheesh! Because you carry her heart? Does she know that?"

"And let her know she has that much control over me? Not a chance." I ran my fingers through my hair in frustration. "She is my biggest weakness now. If she gets killed, I will die. I need to protect that damn girl. Assuming I don't fight off the urge to kill her myself first."

Chez whistled. "Your enemies will have a field day."

"That's why they're not going to find out." I gave him a dark glare. "If word spreads, I'll know it's you and *I* will cut off your head. Body or no body."

Chez put up his paws as if in defeat. "Mum's the word, my friend."

I was going to turn and leave but I stopped first. "Chez."

"Yes?" He was preoccupied with his ball of yarn.

"Are we really friends?"

The yarn ball fell and bounced low on the floor.

Chez's gaze met mine. He didn't seem to be quite sure what to make of me. But he narrowed his solemn gaze and nodded noncommittally. "If you like."

I merely grunted in response before walking away.

Across the grand staircase and to the left of the hall, I was going to walk past Allie's suite but stopped short at the open doorway.

Allie sat on one end of the plush fabric day couch with a bottle of antiseptic and a pile of clean bandages beside her. The Duchess had provided them to replace the 'atrocious scraps of cloth' we had used to bind her wounds.

I didn't have enough magic to heal her injuries either. But I wasn't much inclined to ask the Duchess for any more favors, in case she asked another one of me—the nature of which I already knew I wouldn't be able to grant.

Her lab coat was draped over the armrest. Her sleeves folded up, Allie muttered as she struggled to apply the medicine to her injuries, cursing every so often.

Already shaking my head, I marched over to take the bandages out of her hands.

"I can do it myself." Allie shrugged me off, but her frustration was obvious as she attempted to re-dress her shoulder wound.

She was so bloody stubborn.

Exasperated myself, I brushed her hand aside and gripped her other arm. "I know you can," I said, my tone firm as I sat down beside her. "But let me."

Surprised, those honey-brown eyes gazed up at me, half in suspicion, half in...wonder. She stopped her protest and let me tend to her wound. The bleeding had stopped but it would still need a bit of my magic to heal it completely tomorrow.

I quickly checked her aura. Despite her injuries, she was relatively unharmed. But as I worked, I could sense a certain level of confusion in Allie.

She wasn't sure what to make of me right then either.

She definitely wasn't pleased about our failed quest. She was conflicted about being here. A deep wanting of home burned inside her, but it was marred by frustration since she couldn't remember anything about it.

Having never had to process feelings before, everything only felt jumbled to me. Much noise without a thread of melody. A cacophony of notions without a shred of sense. I shook off the connection.

"It's done." I turned to put the leftover bandages away.

The neckline on my shirt pulled at my skin as it was tugged to one side with Allie peering closer.

I recoiled. "What the hell are you doing?"

She gave me a pointed look. "Your shoulder injury also needs looking at. Take off your shirt."

Shrugging her hand off, I dismissed it. "Leave it. I'll fix it tomorrow with a spell once my magic recovers."

Allie made a face. "It looks horrible. Come on. I'm a doctor, remember?"

"You said you're not that kind of doctor," I reminded her.

She pursed her lips in insistence. "At least let me put the healing balm from the Duchess on it." She leaned forward to inspect my shoulder and I stiffened in my seat.

With excruciatingly slow movements, Allie reached into my shirt from the opening at the neck to apply the balm against my stab wound. Luckily, I had already cleaned it up. I was sure it looked more gruesome earlier.

I glared at the top of her head, of half a mind to push her off and away.

Her hair smelled like...like... I wrinkled my nose as the

realization struck me. The flowers... That intoxicating scent was coming from Allie's hair.

Dammit. I should get up.

"I should go sit somewhere else," I grumbled but I couldn't make my body move away. Allie was warm, soft... Her mere presence seemed to quiet much of the conflicted rage in my head. I was tempted to sink into the couch beside her but my back remained stiff. "This is...odd."

Allie groaned. "What is the big deal? Stop being such a big baby." To support herself, her other hand was propped firm on my other shoulder. Her small hand pressed warm through the fabric of my shirt and sent shivers up my spine.

The way she was leaning over me was bringing her face quite close to mine. I only needed to lift my hand and I could plunge my fingers through that thick mass of silken hair and grasp the nape of her neck to pull her in and take that mouth—

Rolling my eyes in annoyance at my own ridiculous notions, I averted my gaze to look out the window.

A small flock of birds squawked as they flapped across the lagoon behind the Duchess's house. The moon's reflection was full and round among the lilies floating in the still water. Crickets chirped in the humid air. Fireflies dotted the dark gardens.

A snort of laughter escaping Allie startled me from my reverie.

I gave her a wary look. "What?"

"Nothing." She bit her lip. "The uh...Duchess was telling stories about your dalliances back in the day. The story with the pineapple in particular was quite amusing. She refers to your...*gift*," she ventured the word, "as something kind of big, powerful, and dangerous."

I huffed. "If it worked on you, I wouldn't have to bother explaining it."

Allie rolled her eyes. "It's just that it's all so superficial."

I shrugged. "Either way, it works. That's all I care about. It's my job."

She paused from her task. "So, how do you do it? You know, seduce all of those women," she prompted. "Is it a spell?"

I shot her a look.

For the briefest of moments, I thought her gaze dropped to my mouth. "I'm curious."

"Sometimes..." I mumbled. "Sometimes I cast a spell. Sometimes I just look into their eyes. Sometimes it takes a kiss..." I couldn't help my own gaze dropping to her mouth.

Tamping down an irrational urge to move closer, I took a slow, deep breath. "But as we've already established, for some reason, the spell doesn't work on you, so there's no way you would understand."

Her eyebrow rose. "So you've actually cast this spell on me before and it didn't work?"

Meeting her gaze once again, I gave her a pointed, mocking look. "Are you in love with me yet?"

Those red lips quirked up in amusement. "No..." A wistful faraway look crossed her face, hinting at remorse, even embarrassment. "I don't fully remember but...I feel like it's always been like that with me though. I don't think I'll ever *truly* give my heart to anybody."

A gratifying spark of satisfaction, of self-assuredness warmed my chest. I studied the curve of her smooth cheek, that graceful neck, the way her hair tumbled over her shoulders. "But...I stole your heart. Doesn't that make it mine?"

Those honey-brown eyes snapped over to meet my languid prompting gaze in surprise. She scoffed in mocking to recover, taking my statement as if it was a joke. "Yeah. Right."

Turning her attention back to treating my wound, she cleared her throat. "So do you miss your clock tower? This whole swamp is a bit dreary, isn't it?"

My skin prickled under her butterfly touch. She was stroking the balm in circles to even it out, wary not to press too hard on my injury. Slightly disoriented, I grunted noncommittally.

"Chez said you hadn't been across the river in a long while," she went on, not waiting to hear my responses to her questions. "I don't know. It felt more normal to me there. Without the magic."

Almost offended again, I narrowed my eyes. "What sort of mad world do you come from anyway? There's no magic at all? None whatsoever?"

"Well, nothing like what I've seen you do, that's for sure. But I suppose there are other kinds of magic in my world."

"Like what?"

Her eyes clouded over. "I can't...explain it right now. But I feel like...there is." She paused to give her head a brisk shake as if to clear it. "There." Finishing up with my wound, she moved to sit back on the couch. With a deep sigh, she leaned her head against my uninjured shoulder, shifting her head near the hollow of my neck, likely involuntarily.

I could imagine she was exhausted from the day's events and injuries certainly didn't help fatigue.

My shoulder was getting stiff from the awkward angle of her leaning against me. I sighed in resignation and put my arm around her shoulders. "You need to rest."

Somehow she melted against me. "It's already a struggle to fall asleep without the ticking of the big clock. I guess I'd gotten used to it. It's...soothing, I guess." A faint wave of calm was slowly working its way through her aura. A relief. A settledness. She blinked as though trying to keep awake but her eyelids were drooping. "Your world is indeed amazing. I wonder what it was like before... before all this... before you lost your..."

Her mumbling turned incoherent and then she passed out.

I shook my head. I could barely remember the days when I didn't have to put up with an annoying helpless trouble-seeking female mortal. She didn't even realize how lucky she was. In her helpless state, without me to protect her, she would have been completely vulnerable.

Once she was quietly snoring, I set Allie down across the couch properly before straightening up. Her hand was resting slack on her chest, where her heart ought to be. The moonlight shone on her messy hair that had fallen partway across her forehead.

Checking the urge to find a blanket to cover her with, I spun around to leave.

I still needed to do some meditation to regenerate my magic with the overnight tides, and I couldn't do that with her around to distract me.

It seemed instead of indulging in her usual lengthy morning

breakfast feast, the Duchess wanted to personally see us off. By the time I came out of my suite, she was at the front porch, Allie's hand clasped in hers.

Tilting my head to peer at them out the big windows, I slid my hand along the staircase railing as I descended.

Energetic from being once again completely healed from her injuries, Allie ventured her last-minute questions—respectful and curious. "Madame Duchess, if you wouldn't mind my asking..."

The Duchess interjected right away, "Why do I want to die?" She let out an airy laugh. "Darling, I have lived a long, long, *long* life." Her face paled, her skin wrinkling, her entire aura dimmed as she spoke, "My sole purpose has always been to serve the Queen of Hearts. I only move when she says. I only breathe when she says. Such a life is not worth living."

"I see." Allie nodded, her forehead creased in deep thought. "That's...quite interesting."

"Interesting because Rabb has the same purpose and yet, he doesn't feel as I do?" the Duchess prompted.

"Exactly."

Chez popped up and moseyed over to lie out on the porch steps to sun himself.

Glancing at the cat, the Duchess's smile was wan. "Rabb is...a little bit younger than I. And while his emotions have been all but stripped away, I still have a small piece of my Heartfire ember. It seems that to be able to do what I do for the Queen, I must have a certain measure of emotions." She tapped her chest. "I feel sadness. I feel grief. I feel loneliness. I feel guilt. When you get to be as old as I am, all alone, carrying this burden, I imagine you would wish for the end to come swiftly as well."

At her admission, a twinge in my own chest stung for a moment. I supposed some people would find that between the two of us, the Duchess had the worst deal of it. I was almost certain that Allie would think so too.

Allie's frown deepened. "I am so sorry."

"Ah, it is not for you to be sorry about. This is simply the way things are." The Duchess waved it away. A sparkling mist surrounded her hand for a moment until the mist formed into a crystal hand mirror. "Here." She handed Allie the gilded hand mirror.

"What is this?"

"A looking glass."

Allie turned over the delicate glittering accessory in her hand. "Yes, but what is it for?"

"This looking glass will allow us to communicate across the river," the Duchess said, her gaze turning wistful and far-away. "I think I shall miss my new friend. It has been such a long time since I've had quite intriguing company."

Coming out of the French doors, I gave the Duchess an acknowledging nod then held my hand out to take the looking glass from Allie so I could shrink it and keep it in my pocket.

The Duchess clucked her tongue. "Even though it may otherwise seem as though you've made this trip for nothing."

"Not at all." Allie shook her head. "It was very lovely to meet you, Madame Duchess."

"I am sorry I couldn't be of more help." The Duchess's smile quirked a bit as she regarded Allie with a look. "But perhaps I could make you an offer instead. What would you say to your coming to stay here at my estate?"

Allie's mouth dropped open. "What?"

Surprised, I jerked in my stance. On the one hand, I almost sighed in instant relief at the prospect of being unburdened of Allie's infuriating company. But then suspicion struck me.

Was the Duchess trying to hold Allie hostage to coerce me into ending her life? Had the Duchess become aware of Allie's true nature? Was the Duchess trying to take advantage and extract the *coeur* for herself? Did Chez tell the Duchess what she was?

I cast a glance over at Chez but he merely rolled over with a soft purr, not even paying the rest of us any mind.

The Duchess went on. "This big house is too quiet all by my lonesome. And perhaps with your company, I might think of wanting to die less. Plus, you might even get to fixing the cooktop and the steam baths." She peered at Allie's face with a solemn entreat. "If you find your home is much out of reach, I fancy you might have a place here."

Almost startling Allie, I stepped in front of her before the words of offer even settled. "Out of the question, Duchess." I glared at her. "I told you she is mine."

The Duchess raised her hand to her throat. "Ah, my dear Rabb, I stake no claim on her. I was just perhaps thinking that it would be easier on you if she wasn't around. You know I would protect her with all the magic I have." She peered around me to meet Allie's gaze again to promise. "I swear it. You would be safe here."

I didn't glance back to check for Allie's reaction.

The Duchess's trustworthy eyes and earnest nod indeed

rang sincere but the tightness in my chest warred with my sudden headache. It was taxing to think through the reason why but I already knew my answer. I couldn't let the Duchess control my weakness. "No. She'll come back with me and I'll hear nothing more about it."

Eyebrow raising half in amusement, the Duchess pursed her lips. "Whatever you say, Rabb."

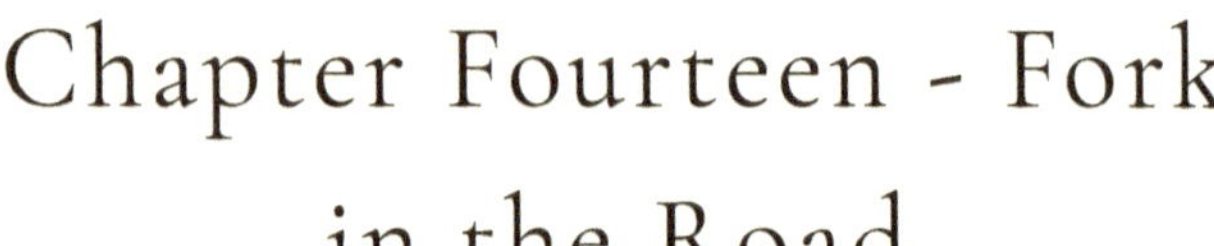

Chapter Fourteen - Fork in the Road

Following Chez as he escorted us away, I strode down the worn lane in the forest just beyond the Duchess's estate where the road forked three ways. Wooden signposts nailed to a tree offered several conflicting suggestions—Hatter's House, Wünder Bog, This Way, Not This Way.

"So which way do we go from here?" Allie studied the signposts closely as the carved letters on the rough surface slipped and changed to intermittently form gibberish.

"Well, that depends where you want to go, of course." Chez hung upside down from a low tree branch. "It doesn't matter which direction you go if you don't know where you're going." The cat's body seemed to disappear for a moment.

Allie rolled her eyes. "Thanks for the cryptic message, Chez."

His yellow-moon grin reappeared first. "This path loops around back to the Duchess's estate. The March Hare's house is that way." A fuzzy paw pointed a paw the opposite way. "And in that direction lives the Hatter with the tree hollow. Of course, he's as mad as they come."

Allie sighed. "I think I may have had just about enough of madness."

"Well, you can't help that," Chez put in. "We're all mad here. I'm mad. You're mad. Rabb is *almost always most definitely* mad."

"Sadly, no argument there." Allie craned her neck to peer down the lane that looped back around.

I furrowed my eyebrows. Was she considering going back to the Duchess? Had she been considering the Duchess's offer from earlier to stay? She did want to be rid of me just as much as I did her. But should I have asked her first?

I cleared my throat. "Did you...want to stay with the Duchess?"

Fidgeting in her stance, Allie bit her lip. "She really seemed quite lonely. I felt sorry for her."

My stomach turned hollow with unease.

"But then it occurred to me you were probably lonely too, all these years alone."

"I wasn't alone," I pointed out, almost defensively. "Even the Duchess has companions and servants. Tell her, Chez."

Glancing back, Chez's eyes widened a bit but he didn't seem to want to contribute. "Oh, oh sure."

"I reckon it's not the same as true intimacy with a person," Allie pointed out. "I suppose you're lucky if you don't have these feelings and were fixed to live forever. But some people need that closeness."

"Not me," I declared, stalking past her to turn toward the lane leading to the Hatter's house.

"This is as far as I go." Chez mocked a salute at us with his paw.

Allie nodded. "I'll look forward to your next visit to the clock tower."

I shot the cat a look. "I won't."

Not in the least offended, Chez shook his head. "Be careful at the Hatter's house," he bid. "I know he used to be a brilliant man, but since the incident with the Dormouse, he's been a bit more unhinged than normal. Keep your wits about you." He wiggled his whiskers, his words trailing off as his purple body disappeared with a pop. "Or else you'll be stuck in his eternal tea party..."

"Thanks, Chez. See you on the other side." Allie gave thin air a casual wave before turning to follow me.

I had to admit I was a bit apprehensive. The Hatter had been a brilliant man. In certain circles, he was known as the Guardian of Doors though I wasn't exactly sure why. Even with the little I knew of him, I was certain he would have a hundred and one uses for a *coeur* if he ever got his hands on one. It wasn't far-fetched to think that he might just be clever enough to figure out what Allie was.

Still, there was no other way across the River of Tears. I pushed some low tree branches out of my way. The Hatter's quaint gray house was already peeking between the foliage as we approached. The dirt lane turned into a narrow cobblestone path.

Allie skipped in her step. "I can't wait to meet this Hatter person. Is he hot like you?"

I almost tripped over my own feet.

Hot. Like. Me?

She met my bewildered gaze. "What? I suppose the Duchess did have a point. I mean, you know you are quite good-looking, objectively speaking. Both your stature and muscle ratio are impressive. And I'm already assured you have incredible stamina—"

A sudden shiver shot up my spine.

"I do live in the room beneath yours. I could hear you, remember?" She put her hands up. "Don't worry, it didn't sound bad. Like I said before, it sounded like those women were greatly pleasured—"

I whirled around to growl. "Enough!"

Stopping in her tracks, she merely blinked at me. "You know." She shrugged. "Kudos."

I clenched my jaw.

Why? I studied the light in her hazel eyes, the hint of a smirk on that mouth, the steadiness of her countenance. Why did I not intimidate her at all? It was infuriating.

Turning away with a huff, I mumbled, "I think you *are* mad."

She threw her hands up. "Chez did say we're all mad here."

Scoffing, I pushed past the metal gate flanking the garden and glimpsing movement to the right, I glanced over.

Morning tea had been set up in the middle of the garden. Mismatched chairs encircled a long, ornate table adorned with a mishmash of teapots, cups, and saucers. The setting seemed almost deliberately disordered with a vibrant and eclectic assortment of tableware and curious decorations. Teacups filled with what appeared to be custard or soup, which seemed to occasionally change in color, and an array of pastries and cakes scattered across the table, their sizes and shapes defying the usual convention.

A small figure busied himself moving from one chair to the next whilst mumbling under his breath.

The Hatter was a homunculus of a man with wiry red hair, sticking all out of his oversized top hat. Dried flowers and herbs adorned his dusty overcoat, with ruffles bursting out of each sleeve. Beady green eyes glowed beneath round horn-rimmed glasses on his wrinkly face, sunken cheeks, and sharp cheekbones.

He was a vision for nightmares. Nobody would doubt his sanity. Where the line between genius and insanity blurred, he was the line.

I cleared my throat. "Mr. Hatter, we—"

The Hatter waved his hand erratically as he yelled, "Please! Please, sit. I haven't had company in such a long while."

Allie met my gaze warily but moved to approach the table.

Seeing Allie's eyes light up at the spread of decadent, mouthwatering food, I almost couldn't help a shake of my head in knowing mirth.

Allie pulled out one of the leather seats.

"Not there!" the Hatter screamed at her and she jumped in alarm. "Those seats are for ghosts," he relayed. "You can't see them now. But they'll be back later. Don't be rude. Change places!"

Wincing as she watched his reactions, Allie slid to the far

end of the table and sunk into a chair. She looked relieved when he didn't yell at her again.

"Please! Help yourself!" The Hatter gestured toward the table.

I sat in the seat beside Allie's but didn't bother to sample the food. "Mr. Hatter, we seek your assistance to—"

"No!" the Hatter snapped. "No business. Tea first."

I sighed in exasperation. Oh, this was going to be torture.

"He said help yourself." Allie gave me a shrug as she reached for several things at once.

"Excellent. Excellent." The Hatter rubbed his hands together. "I am sure the ghosts will be delighted to have company today as well. They lead such dull lives, you know."

Fascination evident in her eyes, Allie dipped a strawberry into her tea. "Very interesting, Mr. Hatter." Munching on a biscuit, she leaned over to whisper to me, almost conspiratorially, "Tastes like waffles."

One corner of my mouth couldn't help but curl up before I could fix my face. I cleared my throat once more as I sank back against my chair, folding my arms across my chest.

"Be careful, my dear," the Hatter piped up. "Strawberry stains on white lab coats are the worst."

Allie's nod was emphatic. "Aren't they? Some days, I'd rather spill nitric acid than a berry extract in my lab."

The Hatter's green eyes lit up. "Ah! Wonderful! You know, I'm somewhat of a scientist myself."

Allie's eyes widened eagerly. "Oh, excellent! What is your field of expertise?"

The Hatter's sudden faraway gaze averted to one side.

"Time. Time is my friend—or he used to be. We quarreled just last March."

"Fascinating," Allie couldn't help but murmur. She seemed entranced by the Hatter's rambling.

"Leap years for example," the Hatter exclaimed with a shake of his head. "They don't make any sense."

"I could not agree more." Allie nodded as she poured maple syrup into her tea before dunking another biscuit in.

"There are two hundred billion trillion stars in the entire universe. When light from a distant star travels a long way, it becomes infrared—which is ironic. Shorter wavelengths are stronger, they carry more heat, but these waves are more of an indigo-violet shade. Do you like colors?" the Hatter prompted.

Allie made a face. "I used to like rainbows. I don't anymore."

The Hatter tapped a finger on his chin in deep thought. "Why is the afterlife like a ball of string?"

"Hmm...I've never heard of that analogy," she mused out loud. "I know there's a theory that the *universe* is made up of vibrating strings or even sheets of paper." She paused to think it over. "Why *is* the afterlife like a ball of string?"

The Hatter turned to her in surprise. "I don't know. Is that your theory? Can you prove it?" He leaned over the table, his tie dipping into his teacup.

Confused, Allie winced. "How might I prove it? You're the one who proposed the notion."

"That's enough with the riddles, Hatter," I snapped. "Can you help us or not?"

"Can I? That's a good question." He rubbed his chin. "'Would I' is an even better one. 'Why should I' even more so."

Straightening up in my seat, I spoke to ensure he understood we would not be diverted by his stalling. "We seek a tree hollow to cross back to the desert."

Tilting his head, the Hatter nodded. "Ah, I see, I see. I know precisely what you seek. Come. Follow me." Standing, he beckoned us to follow him.

Deeper into his garden, the grass was more wild, overgrown. Leaves and twigs crunched underfoot. We passed an armchair turned about before an unlit outdoor fire pit.

The Hatter gave a casual wave of his hand. "You'll have to excuse the March Hare. He hasn't been lively since the incident with the Dormouse."

I glanced over too late.

When Allie's gaze fell on the rotting creature in the chair, skull with sunken eyes, and marred flesh, she jumped, grabbing my arm with a gasp. She turned her face into my chest, her eyes squeezing shut in shock.

Swallowing hard, I put my arm around her shoulders to lead her away. I frowned at her slight tremble and held her a bit closer.

The temperature kept dropping as we walked along the gardens to the back.

The Hatter pushed open another squeaky gate. It led to the forest behind his house. A thick cloud cover dimmed the crisp air. This place was nothing like Tulgey Woods or the swamp surrounding the Duchess's estate. A thin layer of snow covered all the plants. With the low fog, I could barely see more than a few yards away.

And as soon as we stepped through the gate, the sky turned suddenly to dusk, even when in the tea gardens before, it had only just been mid-morning.

Narrowing my eyes in wariness, my gaze shifted around. "Where's the tree hollow, Hatter?"

"Go on then. Off with you." The Hatter shooed us with a wave of his arm.

All around us, about a dozen gray headstones, set out in a haphazard order across the grass, materialized out of the fog.

We had walked into a graveyard.

It seemed the Hatter was indeed the guardian to many doors, including perhaps one to the underworld.

The Hatter sniffed. "I only help people. Ghosts can have tea but nothing else."

My eyebrows furrowed at his sentiment. Was he referring to Allie?

Allie blinked in surprise. "I'm not a ghost."

The Hatter pointed a crooked finger at her. "She's no heart. She's a ghost."

Oh, for god's sake. I gritted my teeth. "I carry her heart, preserved in my chest. She's still alive, Hatter. She's not a ghost."

"Prove it."

15

Chapter Fifteen - Ghosts

"Prove what?" I exchanged a confused glance with Allie.

"That it is indeed her heart you carry in your chest. That she is not a mere ghost." The Hatter folded stubborn arms across his chest. For a little man, he was quite staunch, I'd give him that.

Letting out an exasperated sigh, I motioned Allie closer. "Come here. Give me your hand."

"Why?" Allie pursed her lips but reached out her hand tentatively.

I clicked my tongue, beckoning her over. "Just give it."

Allie took a step closer to me and reached one hand out.

I lifted her hand and touched her palm against my throat, just above my chest. The warmth of her fingertips on my bare skin almost seared my neck.

"Does it beat, girl?" the Hatter wanted to know.

Allie almost gasped as the heart in my chest beat faster

under her touch. A white light began to glow from my chest beneath her palm. Her wide-eyed gaze met mine in surprise. When she dropped her hand, the white light vanished.

The Hatter gave a satisfied nod. "Only the owner of the heart would be able to call upon it. Fascinating. Then you are not of the beyond."

Allie scoffed in incredulity. "Yes. I am still alive. Obviously."

The Hatter approached Allie as if to peer at her closely.

When the Hatter spoke again, my blood ran colder than the weather. "I sense power." He sniffed the air around Allie, his statement directed at me. "Not your mediocre sorcery. I sense...a significance."

I clenched my jaw. I knew the Hatter would be able to sense it. But I also knew it wouldn't do me any good to fight the old man. We were likely evenly matched.

I might be the most powerful sorcerer in Wünder, but it appeared the Hatter held mystical powers of the beyond.

He controlled time and served ghosts tea.

"Look," I began calmly. "There is no need to take this somewhere neither of us wants to go. We will leave peacefully if you just point us to the tree hollow."

The Hatter's eyes held a dark glimmer. "But you ask a favor. In the interest of fairness, perhaps I give you something and you give me something in return."

Seething, I was going to surge forward to scuff him but Allie caught my arm.

Allie met my gaze for a moment before looking to the Hatter. "Perhaps we could make a deal?"

My expression grim, I growled under my breath, "He's not taking you."

"Not me," she corrected. "The Hatter strikes me as a rational man," she declared out loud to compliment the Hatter. "A man of science and many other fine pursuits. Surely, there should be something else we can offer him." She met the Hatter's gaze again. "Isn't there, Mr. Hatter?"

"Something else, you say?" Studying the two of us, the Hatter chewed on his bottom lip. "How about a game? Let's have some entertainment for the lively ones." He clapped his hands.

I frowned. "What sort of game?"

"Ah!" He held up a finger, his eyes lighting up. "There is a treasure. In one of the hollows. You will know it when you see it. If you find it—ah, if you succeed in attaining it, I will give you this treasure." He raised his arm to point a wrinkly finger toward one of the thick trees past a handful of tombstones. "You may begin there."

"What's the catch?" I raised a knowing eyebrow.

"Ah, see. The game is only fit for one."

"Fine." I stepped forward.

Allie tugged on my arm again. "Wait. It makes more sense for me to go."

"How exactly does that make more sense?"

"If you go, and you get in trouble, I don't think my knowledge of advanced nuclear physics will help you out. I should go."

I groaned. "Oh god. I'm going to have to rescue you again, aren't I? Why is it that every time you have an idea, I always end up getting hurt?"

"Bad luck?" She gave me a sheepish grin.

I rolled my eyes. "Oh, great, are you a statistician now

too?" I leaned closer to make my point. "I told you before, your life is precious to me. I cannot have you risking your life for any reason."

"I'm not going to die," she insisted.

Her arrogant, self-assuredness in risking her own life grated on my nerves. "You don't know that."

Allie threw up her hands. "It's just a game, Rabb. I'm sure it's going to be—"

Frustrated, I ran my hands through my hair. "You don't understand—" I burst out, "I just want to live!"

My outburst gave Allie pause. The gears in her head were spinning again. "Wait." She blinked slowly. "All this time, you kept saying you needed me alive. But...are you saying that you actually mean...if I die, you die too?" Her gaze slid to my shoulder and then to the many cuts on my arm. Her forehead creased as if the weight of the truth dawned on her just then. "I didn't expect that."

I averted my gaze. I supposed she could be thinking back to all the instances when it had looked like I was looking out for her well-being. She would be reframing the situation in her mind, why it seemed like I was taking care of her—the only proof she'd held that I cared enough not to harm her, to protect her. In fact, I was only looking out for my own well-being. There was a dull ache in the heart in my chest as the truth sank.

"Yoo-hoo!" The Hatter waved his hand, a wide grin on his face. "Come now and let's start the game. The tea will get cold."

Allie glanced back at him. "What happens if I fail to find this treasure of yours?"

The Hatter clicked his tongue as if aghast. "Fail, my dear? Think not of it. Why, if you do not succeed, then instead we shall celebrate your unbirthday! And you may stay here as my assistant." He shrugged. "Who knows? You might find a place here." He clapped his hands again. "Now the ghosts will want their party. Are you two quite decided?"

"Yes. I'll go." Allie's voice was clear, steady.

I shook my head. There was little point in arguing.

She walked on without further ado, without even a backward glance.

To her credit, I didn't sense fear in her aura. Her heart remained steady in my chest. As usual, all I could feel from Allie was a burgeoning curiosity about what was going to happen next. Such a level of curiosity, of reckless courage, would no doubt do her ill eventually.

Allie tiptoed across the grass, the fog swirling around her ankles as she made her way toward the large tree hollow amidst the garden graveyard.

As soon as she stepped past the dark spiral within the trunk of the tree, the hollow grew in size to accommodate her.

I peered through the burrow, past Allie's figure as the growing doorway allowed a peek into a long, well-lit space. A hallway lined with different sizes and colors of doors.

"It's a hallway of doors..." Allie trailed off, her voice like an echo. Walking past the first two doors and a little chair by the side, she craned her neck. "Oh my god, Rabb." She pointed to the next teak door as she bent to peer through the small window. "This door looks like it leads to your desert. This place must be like a portal corridor!"

Relief settled in my chest.

Finally. Good news.

Glancing down, Allie began to fiddle with her collar.

What is she... I squinted to see and stopped short.

The necklace around Allie's neck was glowing green.

It was that strange contraption that detected spaces and worlds that Allie had been testing in her lab.

All I need to do is find an intersect—a doorway... And once I do, I'm sure I'll find a portal that leads all the way home...

The heart in my chest began to pound.

Allie's gaze slid to the burnt orange door right next to her with another little peephole and bent down to look through.

I swallowed past the lump in my throat.

Her breath caught in her throat at whatever she was seeing through it.

Could she be right? One of the doors was a way back to Allie's strange world?

Excited, Allie rapped on the door. "Rabb, I think this door leads back to my home. This is it! This door must be my way home." Dropping her gaze, she murmured her analysis, "I suppose before, I must have somehow fallen through one of these and ended up here in Wünder." Her voice nearly squeaked in her eagerness, as though everything was falling into place.

The Hatter had a sly sort of smile on his face.

"Is that the treasure?" I pressed him. There was no telling what sort of tricks the Hatter could be playing. Allie could be walking straight into a trap. "Did she find it? Did she succeed?"

Allie was turning and rattling the doorknob to no avail. "It's locked." She blew out a breath and cast her eyes around. Looking upward, she stopped short. "There's a gold key on top of that giant glass table. Is that the—" She sucked her breath in again, her eyes widening even further. Pointing to the other end of what was above her, she cried out, "There's a Heartlamp up there!"

My eyebrows snapped together. What? I slid the Hatter another glance. What the hell was he playing at?

"Allie!" I called out, tamping down the urge to run in there. "What do you see?"

"I think I see a Heartlamp! It's on a ledge against the ceiling. It looks just like the one you used before at that kingdom, Rabb. I'll try to get it." Stepping back from the doors, she dragged the chair toward the center of the room so she could get higher.

My stomach turned. Allie had abandoned her task to grab the key to the door—her only way to get home, to fetch the Heartlamp for me instead.

A shuffling noise reached my sensitive ears. I glanced to one side, straining to hear, before I shot the Hatter another look. "What is that ruckus?"

The Hatter's eyes had glazed over. "Ghosts."

My eyes widened in alarm.

Surrounding the tree hollow Allie had gone through, shadowy figures emerged from beneath the ground, from beneath the tombstones around the backyard garden cemetery. Delicate white flakes of snow started falling from the sky.

"Time for tea," the Hatter remarked with glee.

My eyes darted back and forth between the throng of ghosts and Allie still trying in vain to reach the Heartlamp propped upon the ledge. She didn't seem to hear the dreadful sounds of the ghosts, bones creaking, gnashing of teeth, rattling of invisible chains...

I clenched my jaw. "Dammit Hatter," I demanded. "What's the solution? How does she get up to fetch the Heartlamp? Is there perhaps some sort of hidden potion or trick food to make her grow in size—what?" I shook my head in confusion. "Besides that, how do you even have an activated Heartlamp?"

"That's what the Dormouse asked too before...before..." He trailed off, his face turning pale.

The ghosts were almost up to Allie. They were in the hallway of doors.

I grabbed the Hatter by his shoulders and shook him. "Snap out of it, Hatter. Tell me the solution. How does Allie win the game?"

A cackle tittered out of the old man as he met my gaze. "She doesn't, my good man."

An icy chill gripped me immediately. "What the hell do you mean? What does Allie need to do?"

"This was never about the girl, sorcerer assassin." He gave me a sly smirk.

Stunned, I shoved him away and stepped back. "What?" Clenching my fists, I whirled around enraged. "What the hell are you playing at, you mad old Hatter?"

"I was never after the *coeur*, dear boy. This test was for you. You are one of the more fascinating specimens I've ever encountered. Your assassin aura is changed and I was curious. I wanted to try an experiment."

I swallowed my unease. "What experiment?"

His grin was faint. "To see if you would run in there to save her life."

My gaze returned to Allie as the first lot of the ghosts began to surround her figure. "Save her life? Is she in danger? Is she going to die?"

"Oh, most certainly. Only people with hearts can venture into the underworld unscathed. Those with no hearts will end up frozen in death's sleep."

The heart in my chest began to pound as the ghosts swirled around Allie. For mere wisps of air, they were quite capably thrashing her about. Trying to cover her face, Allie spun and spun as she tried to push back and away from the mob of spirits. The frigid weather began to blow into the hollow and the hallway of doors.

With a highly annoyed yelp, Allie whirled around to steady herself on her feet. She swung her arms in an attempt to fight them off, but her powerless fists merely passed through their smoky figures. More shadows arrived to crowd in with Allie trying to fight them off, but she was drowning in the dense gray fog amidst the developing whiteout.

The Hatter waved his arm.

Across the still-dewy green grass, a new cold tombstone shimmered out of nothing. "It seems we must celebrate another unbirthday." There was a catch in his ominous tone as his beady eyes watched me. "Don't worry," he assured. "You should remain quite safe. The shared curse on that heart will not work in the underworld. It won't affect you as long as you stay out here."

Regardless, my throat tightened. I would no longer share Allie's injuries as long as I didn't go to that place inside the hollow? Could the Hatter really have that sort of power?

True enough, I felt no soreness, no hurt, from the ghosts harassing Allie.

I clutched at my chest. Only, I could still feel her feelings. Allie was distressed, afraid, desperate…

Help me…

There was a dull aching in my chest and I dropped my gaze.

The Hatter peered at my face. "Was this not your wish? To be rid of the strange girl once and for all?" he prompted again.

I glanced into the hollow once again. I could no longer see Allie. She was completely overwhelmed by the ghosts. The heart in my chest pounded harder.

Dammit. Damn it all.

Letting out a huff of annoyance, I shot up off the grass and leaped into the burrow. Whooshing past the throng of undead, I skidded to a stop beside where Allie was. Grunting, I knelt by her side, shrugging off the pungent corpses clamoring all over me.

Immediately, ice shot through my veins and a wave of drowsiness threatened to overcome me as Allie's injuries affecting me came as a sudden shock.

Gritting my teeth, I slammed my fist onto the floor and my magic sent out a powerful gust of air around us that blew all the ghosts back with a wave of flurries. I couldn't kill them since they were already dead, but at least the ghosts were repelled by my magic.

Allie was collapsed on the ground, covered by a thin layer of snow, her eyes closed. Her lips were already blue. She wasn't breathing.

If she died, all my magic wouldn't even have a snowball's chance in hell of reviving her.

And because I had swooped in here, instead of staying outside with the Hatter, I would now no doubt subsequently succumb to my own unbirthday.

The Heartlamp was still propped precariously on the ledge. I was going to fetch it but as soon I tried to summon the object with my magic, it whooshed away.

The hallway of doors expanded in length, one end pushing farther away, the gaps between the hallway doors lengthening. Then the hallway moved around us in a circle as bright lights popped up in a colorful whirl and loud whimsical carnival music began to play.

We were stuck in the middle of a merry-go-round. And the ghosts were slowly making their way back to us.

I froze on the spot as a flash of terrifying shadows and screams with the echo of a memory ravaged through my mind once more. I could almost make out the blur of figures in my vision, as though they were people. I couldn't make out any faces but the immobilizing fear was as vivid as anything. It was as if the terrifying memory was happening again right then, triggered by the onslaught of Hatter's ghosts.

My skin chilled in fear, in helplessness. My limbs fell slack, weak, as a painful constriction stabbed in my chest. It was as though my heart was being squeezed before splitting into a thousand tiny pieces.

No! I screamed in my head.

I couldn't let myself get overwhelmed. I had to move. I had to save Allie.

I forcibly shook off the paralyzing cold dread. Steeling myself, I willed my consciousness to return to the present.

The frigid snowstorm blowing through the hallway of

doors. The merry-go-round of tricks. Allie's unconscious body lying on the floor.

Help me...

Narrowing my eyes, I cursed under my breath and tried to spot the teak door from amidst the dizzying, spinning colors.

Unaffected by the merry-go-round, the throng of ghosts began their assault once again, pushing, clamoring, wailing. This time, intent on clouding my view and covering Allie in darkness once more.

The Hatter's cackle rang in the air.

I gritted my teeth in disdain.

Without hesitating further, I scooped Allie up in my arms. With another yell, I summoned another gust of wind. It imploded with a crackle around my form to sweep back another wide circle of the ghostly figures. Then, straining to time my shot correctly, I pointed my finger at the whirling array of doors to target the teak door to my home.

The wooden door shattered into shards, revealing the hollow portal before I jumped backward to fall through it with Allie in my arms.

I caught a glimpse of the Hatter above us, appearing as a tall, looming monster as he watched us from his tea garden. As though we were insects trapped in a giant glass bell jar. He peered down at us—his experiment, with curious eyes.

"Fascinating..." The Mad Hatter's hollow voice echoed as his mad world spiraled in my view. His green beady eyes turned red, glittering fainter and fainter, farther away, until his form was reduced to a tiny black dot, and then nothing at all.

16

Chapter Sixteen - Just a Spell

I crashed backward against a clump of dried bushes. Glancing around quickly, I was relieved to find that we had indeed arrived back at the barren desert beneath my clock tower.

Groaning, I ignored the aching in my back from the impact and secured my grasp around Allie. Immediately shooting upward to fly us to my loft, a simple spell set the metal door to my loft flying wide open.

I hauled Allie's icy figure onto my bed to assess her condition. My shoulders slacked in relief to find she was breathing again.

"Allie?" I called to her. "Wake up. We're back."

"I wanted—a discovery—I'm sorry—"

"Allie?" I frowned.

Somehow, her temperature was still dropping. Her eyes

fluttered open and closed, as if she was floating in and out of consciousness. She tried to shake her head. "It was the only—I had to find—" She mumbled unintelligibly. "Those ghosts—"

I shook my head. "Those ghosts won't harm you now. You almost froze to death—again. You shouldn't have gone to the underworld."

She was delirious. "I'm dead. I died—"

"No, Allie, no. You're alive." Shrugging off my cloak, I tore open the neck of my shirt, took her hand, and pressed it against my bare chest. I winced at the ice of her fingers but murmured deep in my throat, "Feel this. Your heart beats beneath my chest. I am alive. *You* are alive."

I couldn't help my eyebrows furrowing in concern as I looked her over.

Her face was pale, eyes closed, lips blue.

Not much different from when I had first found her frozen in the wastes.

Except...

Heat. She needs heat.

My chest heaving, my gaze pinned on her mouth. Allie's heart pounded harder in my chest as a dull ache tugged at the pit of my stomach. My lips tingled.

It's okay if you want to kiss me... Perhaps if my life depended on it...

I stroked her bottom lip with my thumb. "Allie...you need to get warm."

I bent my head and covered her mouth with mine to initiate a revival spell. The drain on my magic was immediate. Such was the nature of energy transfer magic. Last time, it didn't even occur to me to use this much of my power on her for healing purposes.

But now...

No time to hesitate, I pushed my tongue past her cold lips to give her my heat.

Even as I convinced myself I was doing it to save her life, I couldn't help the rumble in my chest at the taste of her. God, but she was sweet.

The last thing I should be doing was kissing this girl but there was a vague prickling in my chest. I couldn't lose her.

A faint moan escaped Allie. A hint of surrender that lit a fire deep in my soul.

"Yes, Allie." My murmurs against her lips were husky and low. "I am here. Feel me."

It was working. Her fingertips grasped at my neck had warmed considerably.

It was enough.

When I moved to break off, a sting of reluctant protest burned my chest.

But Allie lifted her chin, chasing my lips for more.

God—

A helpless groan pulled from my throat and I dipped my head to capture her mouth all over again.

I grasped the nape of her neck to angle her head to receive my warmth better, in turn deepening the kiss, slanting my lips punishingly hard across hers...soft, pliant.

Another groan tore from my throat when those same fingers slid up into my hair, clutching at me. She was tugging me closer.

Allie's rigid body was warming up, yielding, and my healing spell slowly grew into something else.

Shifting my hard body to cover hers, my insistent lips traced a hot line past her jaw, beneath her ear, down her neck. My nose dug into her hair as I cradled her body against mine. The fragrance of flowers filled my lungs once again. When I shifted again, I couldn't help my hips nestling between her legs.

I groaned yet again. I hadn't had a companion share my bed in a few days. The tug of want deep in my belly was close to unbearable, but somehow, for a change, it was more than her body calling to mine. The aching constriction in my chest was of a different nature. Looking up at her face, I moved my hand to brush her hair back.

I wanted to gaze into those lustrous eyes. I wanted her to give me that derisive look. I wanted her to try to make me laugh again.

I stroked her cheek to whisper, "Allie..."

As if on cue, Allie jerked to sit up with a loud gasp.

Eyes wide, I rolled to avoid smacking our foreheads together and fell off the bed with a hard thump on the wooden floor.

"Ow—!"

Groaning, I rubbed my back as I sat up on the hard floor. I took a few moments to catch my breath, to calm myself down.

Ah, dammit.

I felt...interrupted. I couldn't help the annoyance in my tone. "Was that really necessary?"

Allie's gaze darted this way and that as she got her

bearings. Then she covered her mouth with her hand. That look in her eyes was an easy giveaway. She knew exactly what we'd just done.

She could probably still feel my kiss.

I sure as heck could still feel hers.

I glanced away. "Um…" I debated getting up and walking away if only to escape the discomfort, but this was *my* loft.

She pushed her hair back behind her ear. Her face flaming red, she cleared her throat. "So…that wasn't exactly CPR."

Cracking my neck, I shifted in my seat. "It was a healing spell. Sorry if I—"

"Oh, no, no." Allie waved her hand to dismiss. "I understand. It's fine." Dropping her gaze, she stroked her bottom lip with her finger in deep thought.

"What?" I asked.

I thought her cheeks tinged pink again.

Narrowing my eyes, I prompted again, "What?"

"Nothing, um…" She hesitated. "Remember I kept saying everything in this world tastes like waffles?"

"What about it?" I raised an eyebrow.

"They do though." She nodded. "The Duchess's soup. The Hatter's tea. Everything in this world tastes like waffles to me… Except you."

Swallowing hard, my gaze dropped to her red lips, still plump and swollen…because of me.

Allie had tasted like strawberry tea.

And cloudy days and lost memories…

Before I could stop and wonder if she perhaps liked how I tasted, I shook off the notion.

Ignoring the stir in my stomach, I straightened up. "Either

way, you're still alive. And we made it back. Even with all the shenanigans from that mad Hatter."

Sliding her legs to the side of the bed so she could put her feet on the floor, she bit her lip. "I'm sorry we weren't able to get the Hatter's Heartlamp."

I shook my head. "I reckon there was no way that the Hatter would have let us get that Heartlamp. If indeed it was even a real one to begin with. It's possible many of those things were mere illusions. I think that madman was simply toying with us."

Her face pale, Allie gave a disheartened nod. She understood I was also referring to the alleged doorway back to her home. Her gaze was still on the floor. "Thank you for saving me. Even though, I now understand it's because you were only trying to protect yourself."

I opened my mouth to argue but stopped myself.

Her restless eyes couldn't settle on a spot. Her mind was likely still reeling from everything that had just happened.

I frowned. An unspoken protest weighed on my chest. She didn't know I didn't have to rescue her. She didn't know I could have just let her get mauled by the ghosts. I wanted to explain. I wanted her to really understand...

Allie pushing up off the bed nearly startled me. "I should...probably get some rest," she declared. "Now that I'm..." She trailed off, her voice faltering.

Stuck here, I finished for her in my head as there was a dull thud in my chest. *With me.*

But before I could offer any sort of comfort, she had hurried away to clatter down the spiral staircase.

17

Chapter Seventeen - And Curiouser

The gloomy sunrise brought a vague sense of discontent to my clock tower. Like an empty hollow where conviction used to be.

Beneath my loft where there was always a pervasive insistent indignation since Allie's arrival, I no longer felt restlessness.

Allie's spirit was flat. As though the fight in her had been slowly dissipating and whatever shred of hope she'd been holding on to before was lost.

The overnight tides had come and gone. Through the night, the studio downstairs had been too quiet. I almost thought Allie would have already escaped again.

I already know it's pointless to try to run away from you...

Chewing on my bottom lip, I took a step toward the

spiral staircase then spun back around for the third time in hesitation.

This is ridiculous.

Again, I stared at the tray of food I'd prepared on the little round table. A plate of strawberry waffles with maple syrup. Breakfast.

This is absolutely ridiculous.

She needs to eat, another voice in my head said.

She doesn't need to eat that, a third contradictory voice replied.

She probably didn't want to see me anyway. I imagined she would still have been exhausted from the events of yesterday. Not to mention her almost dying again. She hadn't slept well either.

Frustrated, I buried my head in my hands.

I'd had trouble sleeping too.

Your assassin aura is changed...

The encounter with the Hatter was sludge in my brain. Permeating. Sticky. But I refused to let that madman occupy my thoughts. This was exactly what he wanted. He wanted to mess with my head. And I wouldn't give him the satisfaction.

The unmistakeable sound of glass breaking shattered the strained silence.

Jerking in alarm, I rushed down the stairs and peered into Allie's lab.

Allie was hunched over her work table, her shoulders heaving up and down, her fists clenched white at her sides. Spare metal parts and broken blue glass lay on the table before her. Some scattered on the floor at her feet.

"What happened?" I couldn't help a frown of concern as

I approached. "What are you doing?" I assessed the materials on the table. As near as I could figure, she was making another version of her frequency detector necklace but on a larger scale.

Allie shook her head, her hair hanging down to hide her face. But before I could ask again, her shoulders began to shake as soft, stifled sobs escaped her form.

The heart-wrenching anguish and despair in her stabbed at my chest.

Allie took a deep breath between sobs. "It doesn't work. It's not going to work," she cried. "I'll never get back home. I'm going to be stuck here." She threw up her hands in complete desolation. "I'm going to die. The Queen is going to kill me. If the other terrifying creatures in this world don't murder me first. I don't know what to do anymore. It's too late! I can't—I can't—" She was turning frantic.

Without even thinking, I moved to brace my arms around her, tugging her back against my chest. "Allie, Allie," I soothed into her hair. "You're okay. I've got you. It's going to be okay." She tried to push away but I squeezed her tighter.

"I don't even know who I am," she mumbled. "What if I never remember?"

"I don't care who you were. It doesn't matter to me." Clenching my jaw in determination, I urged, "Look, it's not too late. Maybe you'll find another way home someday. We might find another doorway—or you know, knowing you, maybe you'll build one," I threw in, offhand. I almost didn't recognize my own voice in saying the words. "But until then, I'll protect you. I swear it. You'll be safe."

Her chest heaved as she gave up her struggle.

"Hey," I whispered near her ear. "I mean if you're keen to fight another rainbow, there's always that option. Right?" My eyebrows furrowed, I waited for her breathing to even out.

When she calmed down, she willingly melted in my arms, nestling back deeper against my chest. Heaving a huge sigh, she wiped her face with her hands. "I'm sorry. I didn't mean to disturb you."

I shook my head to dismiss her concern. "You didn't disturb me..."

There was that unfamiliar stir in my stomach again.

Her warmth, that scent...

Almost involuntarily, I bent my head lower ever so slightly to nuzzle her hair with my nose, my lips nearly brushing her ear.

I wanted to get lost in that scent.

Get lost in this moment.

The ticking of the clock around us.

Allie's breathing.

Her softness against my chest...since she wasn't pulling away.

I happened to catch our reflection on the darkened glass wall of the clock tower. My arms were wrapped around her and she quite naturally leaned back against me.

My own mind was so clouded that, try as I might, I couldn't pin down what Allie was feeling right then. What was she feeling? Did she want me to leave but couldn't find the words? Did she want me to stay and keep holding her...?

A loud hiss of steam and a mechanical hum jerked me back to my senses as a bit of machinery came to life across the room.

I squinted. *What the hell—?*

The silent iron-framed cage of an ancient elevator well installed within the corner of the studio looked about the same as it always did—rusty, worn out, inoperable. Except...it was working?

Glimpses of exposed brass pipes and spinning gears passed before my eyes as the elevator car clinked and clanked upward disappearing into the studio ceiling.

My nerves set taut in an impending urge to jump into action once again, I released Allie before striding across the room to climb up the spiral staircase.

Ever curious, Allie followed behind me, peering past my form to see.

The squeaky elevator came to a stop with a slight jolt in the corner of my loft as a purple cat was tugging open the wrought-iron gates.

Upon catching sight of us by the stairs, Chez's eyes lit up. "Oh, hey guys. Did you try out the elevator yet?"

Mystified, I blinked again. "What?" I was still trying to re-surface from the haze of the unexpected onslaught of mixed emotions I had just absorbed.

"Allie fixed your elevator." Chez crossed the floor. "Seri-ously, Rabb. When was the last time you had a walk around? Allie has been fixing all the rickety crumbling parts of this rust bucket clock tower you call a home."

I glanced over at Allie standing beside me.

Eyes wide, she wrapped her arms around herself as though she was trying to ward herself from something, or shaking something off. If I didn't know any better, I would've thought her cheeks were tinged pink again.

Was she relieved about the interruption? Her manner still seemed apprehensive but at least her aura was more settled now than when I'd first gone downstairs.

I shot Chez a dark look. "Don't you have somewhere else to be? I'm busy."

"I'm here to see Allie."

"What makes you think Allie has time to entertain you?" I snapped.

"Um, I think I'll go back downstairs and clean up that mess," Allie said, her face still solemn.

I waved my hand with a bit of a spell. "It's done."

Stopping in mid-stride, Allie shot me a stunned look. "Uh, th-thanks." She wrinkled her nose. Jerking her thumb down the stairs, she mumbled, "Still, I better go make sure nothing blows up again."

"I didn't magic all your stuff away," I called out to let her know. "Just the broken glass mess."

Pursing her lips, she nodded. "Great. Thank you."

I watched her go down the staircase. An inexplicable lightness in my chest, I took a deep breath.

And Chez watched me.

I shot him a look. "What?"

"You look..."

"What?"

Chez shrugged. "Relaxed," he mused. "Having Allie around puts you at ease, doesn't it? I can imagine having you around must put her at ease as well."

My neck burned. The too-recent moment we'd shared downstairs not minutes earlier flashed red hot in my mind.

I looked away to dismiss it. "That's...irrelevant. Why are you here?"

"The Duchess wanted to make sure you all arrived back safe and sound," Chez began. "Do you still have the mirror that she gave Allie?"

I drew out the mirror from my pocket. With a spell from my finger, the gilded hand mirror grew to about as large as a window, propped up against the round table. The Duchess's petite form within it was framed with ornate glistening crystal.

"Helloooo!" Curls bouncing around her round face, the Duchess's melodious greeting sang out as her smiling image waved.

Chez pounced closer, stepping past the plate of waffles. He paused to take a sniff. "Ooh, these look nice."

Frowning, I snapped my fingers and the tray disappeared with a poof. "They're not for you." When I turned back, the Duchess was peering too closely at my face. I nearly jumped back. "What?"

Her big blue eyes were boring into mine. "Your eyes look different," she started. Her breath caught in her throat almost immediately. "Rabb, do you...have your emotions back again?"

Chez clicked his tongue. "You know what, he did say something that sounded quite a lot like jealousy earlier."

I glared at the cat. I rolled my eyes again to dismiss him. "Don't be ridiculous."

"So touchy!" The Duchess's laughter tinkled through the mirror. "In any case, how was your visit with the Hatter?"

Hot frustration rose in my chest, I pursed my lips. "We

almost got trapped there. I *almost* got a Heartlamp. Allie *almost* found a way home."

"Oh." Forehead creasing in concern, the Duchess shook her head. "Allie must be devastated. She told me about all her experiments and that funny contraption she hangs around her neck that helps find other worlds. Where is she?"

I shrugged. "Downstairs. She's probably working on something again."

The Duchess tsked. "That poor girl. Does she still think you'll let her go home once you've drained her Heartfire ember with the Heartlamp?"

I was a little affronted by what I took to be nosy criticism—or perhaps it was a nagging little pang of guilt that I forcibly shook off. The Duchess had no idea what I had to deal with. She had no idea how high the stakes were for me. Then again perhaps she would have rejoiced were she in my position and facing the end of the line. Folding my arms across my chest, I huffed. "That's my business."

A gasp near the spiral staircase grabbed my attention.

Allie was halfway up, her eyes wide in horror.

Oh, for god's sake.

She had been eavesdropping again.

Those honey-brown eyes slid to meet mine, her jaw clenched. "I should have known," she murmured. "I'd thought maybe I could actually trust you to keep your word but you were lying to me this whole time, weren't you?" Her gaze dropped. "You never wanted to help me. You've only been protecting me because, for some reason, you get hurt when I get hurt. But you weren't even going to tell me the truth about this." Her voice shook. "Was the Heartlamp even going to restore my memories or not?"

I cracked my neck in unease. "It would have," I supplied. "But only before it took your life altogether." There was a strange lump in my throat. My own words were bitter in my mouth as if for some reason they revolted me.

Allie's chest heaved. "You've been lying from the start. You were never going to let me go."

My own chest constricted at the look in her eyes. She was right. She *was* right and yet... "Allie." I reached for her arm.

She shrugged me off, scorn burning in her eyes. "You know what, don't even." She shook her head. "I thought we were finally friends. I thought, after everything—after all this—" She broke off, at a loss.

My stomach was hollow. I couldn't stand the cold look in her eyes. The disappointment. The regret.

Squeezing my eyes shut for a moment, I composed myself. "Look." My voice came out dark, deep, and bitter. "I told you from the very beginning. All I needed you to do was to keep quiet, stay out of my way, and stay alive. But no!" I threw up my hands in aggravation. "You keep getting into trouble and trying to escape!"

"Of course, I will!" she retorted. "What makes you think I want to stay here forever?"

I winced. That struck an unexpected chord. "What makes you think I *want* you to stay here forever?" I bit back with a sneer. "You said it yourself. I'm the bad guy. The fact that you expected anything else from me only means you're even more of a fool than I thought."

Allie sucked in a breath as though I'd slapped her with

those words. Her face was crumpled in derision but I could see it on her face. She couldn't deny what I said. She had known what I was right from the start. She just didn't want to admit that she had been fooled.

And I... I needed to remind myself exactly what I was keeping her around for. I needed to remind myself of what I was since it was so very clear in her eyes what I was. I was still a heartless monster.

Even though... I dropped my gaze before I could say anything else I knew I would come to regret.

Still breathless, Allie stood as if in a stunned trance.

"Hoo!" Chez wheezed out loud, instantly breaking the tension. "That was a bit heavy. Now shall we just agree to disagree?"

I glared at Allie. But she merely glared back.

The Duchess glanced from Allie to me and back in expectation. "My..." she murmured.

A sharp knock at the door drew surprised gasps from both Allie and the Duchess.

Jerking in alarm, my gaze snapped over. I wasn't expecting anyone at this time. According to Her Majesty's schedule, she wasn't due another heart for another fortnight.

The knocking came again, firmer, more insistent.

If it was the Hatter come to fight me, I had to get ready. If it was the Queen's envoy come to check up on me, I couldn't let them find Allie in here. No matter her capacity to get under my skin and how much she pissed me off.

Catching Allie's wide-eyed gaze, I put a finger to my lips. Narrowing my eyes in wariness, I approached the door to take a look.

When I cracked the door open to peek outside, there was no one standing at the stoop—except a gust of wind carrying a fresh scroll as it blew straight into my loft.

I stepped back and shut the door again.

The scroll floated in mid-air, glimmering in golden light as it unrolled before us.

The Queen's red seal was at the bottom again.

It was an invitation to the Queen of Hearts's castle.

Chez's ominous tone broke the tense silence. "It's addressed to Allie."

"Oh my," the Duchess cooed again, putting a hand to her throat. "The last time I was invited to the castle to play croquet, the Queen beheaded half the staff and some of the guests for misunderstanding her made-up rules."

"I remember," Chez piped up. "Even *I* almost got beheaded. If only those guards didn't get confused about whether or not they could behead a cat without a body. The Queen's guards are quite dumb."

Allie visibly repressed a nervous shiver.

Another noise at the door turned my head.

An opulent conveyance floated right outside the door to my loft, despite it being about five-hundred feet above the ground. Its stagecoach wheels intricately designed with ornate patterns of suits of cards, the bulbous carriage adorned with flamboyant embellishments in red and black.

Swallowing hard, Allie stepped back. "I don't have a choice, do I? I can't not go. The Queen will find me and kill me either way, won't she?"

Not willing to fib about it, Chez merely shrugged.

I cast her a blank look. Not wanting to expose my own apprehension, I said nothing else except, "Get ready to leave."

"Say hi to Five for me," the Duchess called out to her as Allie headed for the staircase.

Allie glanced back. "Who's Five?"

The Duchess's smile was suggestive. "One of the castle guards."

Allie took a big, deep breath before disappearing back downstairs again.

The impending threat having passed straight over her head, the Duchess covered her mouth in a giggle.

I rolled my eyes at her caprice. I tilted the mirror to cast a spell to shrink it smaller once again.

"Rabb, wait," the Duchess piped up.

I met her gaze.

Her tone turned somber. "Allie's heart..."

I nodded. "I know."

"Do you?" Her curls fell to one side as she tilted her head. "If you recall what I said, the Heartfire ember ignites from the memories of loved ones. *Love*, Rabb," she pressed. "Once Allie's heart fills with memories of love, then all is lost."

I nodded again. "Yes. We just need to make sure Allie doesn't have a chance to recover her old memories before I can get a Heartlamp."

"Ah..." She paused, a catch in her tone. "It need not be past memories. Another way the Queen may possess Allie's heart is if she loves. That is...if she falls for you too."

A shiver ran up my spine. At the implication of her words, my eyebrows snapped together. "Too? What the hell do you mean 'too'?"

The Duchess gave me a half-smirk.

I shifted uncomfortably in my stance, absolutely not keen to dig deeper into the matter. "She's not going to fall for me," I claimed with a soft growl. "She said so before. She doesn't love like that. I can't even seduce her, for god's sake. Nothing I do affects her at all." I couldn't help the frustration in my tone. "Besides, you heard what she said. She hates me. I'm the bad guy, remember?"

The twitch in my chest stung at the recollection of the raw resentment in Allie's eyes. She was *never* going to fall for me.

I clenched my jaw.

But perhaps the Duchess had a point too. There was no telling if Allie would remain immune to my charms and spells.

The stakes were too high to risk the chance.

I needed to focus on my mission.

18

Chapter Eighteen - Queen of Hearts

The entire carriage ride to the Queen's castle was filled with tense silence.

Allie's face was turned out the window as she ignored me. Still upset about having learned the truth.

I couldn't blame her. It was well enough.

She seemed entranced by the cotton candy clouds dotting the sky we flew past.

And I was only so glad not to have to endure her conversation or listen to her ramble on and on about experiments and portals. Even though talking of science always made those hazel eyes light up, always made her aura glow with happiness...

I shook my head to snap out of my reverie.

When the carriage made its descent, the view out the

window turned a lively green. Wheels rattling on the pebbled path, the carriage maneuvered through the castle gardens.

Sprawling with a riot of color and whimsy, rows of meticulously pruned rose bushes bordered intricate mazes of trimmed hedges and manicured lawns. Curious topiaries, sculpted into the Queen's likeness, dotted the trees and columns lining the road.

Allie's eyes rose to the top of the grand and imposing structure we approached.

Towering spires reached toward the sky, topped with flags heralding the Queen's coat of arms gaily waving in the wind of the bright, sunny day. The castle walls were decorated in varying sizes of suits of cards painted in bold, contrasting colors. A heart-shaped wrought-iron gate swung open as flamboyantly attired soldiers marched alongside.

Our carriage stopped right at the wide stone steps leading up to the castle.

A whiff of roses filled the air as the carriage door swung open and a footman arrived to help passengers down.

Allie had only begun to reach out her hand before her gaze fell on the footman. She had to bite down a gasp.

The footman was one of the Queen's headless soldiers. With his boxy uniform, square shoulders, and the number ten emblazoned with a heart on his coat, he almost looked exactly like the playing card decorations adorning the Queen's castle.

I watched Allie's jaw clench as she composed herself.

Her hand moved to take his with no further shake or flutter.

I alighted the carriage by myself.

Their boots clattering on the stone steps, another pair of

uniformed soldiers approached us. With heads this time. The one with the number two on his coat came to inspect us while the one with the number seven stepped up to puff his chest out as he began his declamation.

I almost rolled my eyes. I'd been through this inspection before. Regular citizens of Wünder were often caught out for ridiculous infractions, bringing the wrong color flowers, wearing too-tall shoes—and then beheaded, mostly to amuse the Queen. But for sorcerers like me, there were never any real repercussions. However, the guards would never disobey the Queen's orders, even if she herself had once acknowledged that I was exempt from these pointless proceedings.

"You are about to enter the castle of Her Majesty the Queen of Hearts," Seven decreed. "Rule number one, only speak when you are spoken to. Rule number two, never disrespect the Queen. And rule number three, most essentially, never bother Her Majesty with matters that are wholly important." He stumbled on his words before correcting himself, "Unimportant."

Two agreed with a haughty nod. "It is the oldest rule in the book."

Allie made a face. "Then shouldn't *that* be rule number one?"

Unable to help my amusement, I bit my lip.

Seven winced but he only waved his hand to Two. "Check them for weapons."

Two sniffed around my form and helped himself to check inside the pockets of my cloak. He murmured as he went on, "Tiny looking glass...broken hurricane lamp, pocket watch..."

He glanced at my side. "Dagger—that's a weapon, sir." He moved to reach for it.

Shrugging him off, I cleared my throat.

Two blinked at me.

I gave him a glare. "Try and take it from me."

The guard stepped back as if disoriented, mumbled under his breath again, before turning his attention to Allie. "Miss, please turn out your pockets."

Soldiers with heads didn't seem to intimidate Allie. That or she was taking my cue. She could tell the inspections were mere formality too. She pursed her lips to show the inside of her lab coat pockets. "Just some herbs and powders," she relayed with an attempt at a sweet smile.

Satisfied with our inspection, the two guards led us up the wide stairs and through the giant double doors into the castle.

Allie stared up at everything in wonder. The stained-glass ceiling, the extravagant paintings on the walls, empty metal suits lining the corridors, the vaulted window arches, the thick, red brocade curtains.

Another set of double doors opening up led us straight to the grand throne room.

Even from the entrance, the throne of the Queen of Hearts was already the most imposing feature. Fashioned with ornate, heart-shaped motifs and upholstered in rich, crimson velvet, its backrest rose dramatically with intricate carvings, and gilded accents in even more sculpted heart shapes.

I took a deep breath. We weren't in danger yet. And if the Queen had let us come this far, it was possible she didn't suspect anything. That or she was lulling us into a false sense of security. Either way, I needed to remain vigilant.

It took Allie a few steps through the door to notice that the walls all around us were lined with a distinctly-familiarly-shaped object.

I caught the gasp in her throat when she realized what they were.

Thousands of used Heartlamps decorated the walls of the Queen's throne room, from all the Heartfire embers the Queen had collected, from all the hearts the Queen had ever stolen.

Though all these Heartlamps were empty, spent.

I had heard that the Queen disposed of the spent embers in the massive rock garden in the rear of the palace.

Allie's fists clenched at her sides as we approached the front of the room.

I felt her tension rise, the heart in my chest beating slightly faster.

Despite the contrast in size to her giant throne, the Queen of Hearts's commanding, imperious presence filled the room. It was as though her spirit, her substance, was in everything, everywhere. High collar and crown, both featuring heart patterns, the Queen's resplendent outfit was adorned with red and black playing card motifs, and voluminous skirts billowed dramatically around her seated form.

Her eyes bore a formidable intensity that was both regal and capricious. But there was a touch of whimsy in the slow smile that spread across the Queen's features as Allie and I came closer.

When I moved to curtsy, Allie followed my lead.

"I am sensing apprehension, but not fear," the Queen called out. "I like it." Her tone was amused, disarming. "But you need not fear me. I vow I will not take your heads today." Her smile turned sly as she added, "Or your hearts."

Still wary, my eyebrows furrowed. Obviously, the Queen's promise didn't preclude her intentions from changing for tomorrow.

Allie's manner was just as apprehensive.

The Queen raised an eyebrow to prompt, her gaze pinned on Allie. "You do not believe me, girl?"

Allie curtsied lower. "Apologies, Your Majesty. It's only that I have already been deceived several times since my arrival into your world." Her sharp gaze hinted sideways at me but she didn't look me right in the eyes.

The Queen's smile widened as she glanced from Allie to me and back. "I think I would love to hear stories from the time since your arrival. I regret that my Rabb has not been quite as forthcoming as I had hoped."

Allie straightened up. "Where shall I begin, Your Majesty?"

She waved her hand. "Well, begin at the beginning, and go on until you come to the end, and then stop." She smiled again. "I would be especially curious as well to hear stories of this 'other' world from where I hear you have come from."

Allie grimaced. "I am sorry again, Your Majesty, but I'm afraid I don't remember anything about who I am and where I'm from. I only remember waking up already here in Wünder."

The Queen let out a puff of air between her lips as if in mocking. "Bah. 'Tis quite simple to recover such memories. I can help you if you like?" Her offer sounded much too casual indeed.

Allie paused. "In exchange for what?"

The Queen's melodious burst of laughter echoed throughout the great chambers. "Ah, my dear, I see you are not a stranger to the ways of the world. But I am nothing if not a hospitable hostess. Shall we strike a bargain then?" A glint of glee shone in her eyes at her proposal. "I shall help you restore your memories, but of course, you must also do something for me."

I watched the shadow of caution flicker past Allie's face. "What?" she asked, her tone bordering on dread.

Her pearly white teeth nearly gleaming, the Queen grinned. "Why, you must attend my ball this evening."

Allie seemed to still be waiting for more, for further stipulations. "That's...it? You want me to attend your ball?"

The Queen waved her arm again with a rattle of the beads on her sleeve. "Of course, my dear. That is all I wish."

"That's it? That's all you want?" Allie's forehead was creased.

"Yes. I'm not a monster." The Queen laughed again. "I confess, upon hearing about your plight from a royal courtesan or two, I was struck with the most sincere urge to help you. Perhaps since you are lacking a way home, I can help you find your place here in Wünder." She went on to explain, "You see, my ball is attended by the most elite kingdoms across the land. Surely, we shall find you somewhere you could belong. A suitable kingdom. One that might flourish with your particularly extraordinary uniqueness."

I almost scoffed. The Queen was probably thinking of giving Allie one last night of frivolity and merriment before enacting her malicious plans. I caught Allie's sideways glance almost try to meet mine again. Her trepidation was completely warranted. I resisted the urge to move closer, to put a hand on her shoulder.

The Queen signaled one of the guards again. "If you'll follow Five, he shall lead you to your quarters to freshen up after your journey. Perhaps some refreshments. Tea and scones?"

Allie's eyes started to light up but she suppressed it. She must have been thinking that the food here was intended to poison her anyway.

Casting me yet another wary *almost* glance, Allie let the footman lead her away.

Once Allie had exited the throne room, I folded my arms across my chest and regarded the Queen with a steady look. "It's a trick, of course."

The Queen let out another amused laugh. "My dear Rabb. I swear to you, I have no interest in the girl—or her *coeur*."

I clenched my jaw. So she already knew. And yet she was being this nonchalant. There was obviously something else going on. But there was no way the Queen would reveal her plans to me. I only had to make sure I kept the upper hand.

"I find it hard to believe you really aren't going to take her heart, already knowing it could be a legendary Heartfire ember," I chided.

For a moment, the Queen's gaze glanced down at my chest. She knew exactly where the *coeur* was too. She knew it was not with Allie. But she tilted her head with a mere drawl, "Why do you care? Are you so concerned about this girl? I heard a rumor from the Hatter that you risked your life to save her when you didn't need to."

Keeping my irritation in check, I pursed my lips. "I was only attempting to fetch a Heartlamp, and that Hatter was simply playing tricks on us. He's probably spreading all sorts of lies across Wünder."

"So you don't care about this girl?"

"Like you, I am only interested in the magic of her *coeur*," I declared.

"Excellent." The Queen clapped. "Then we have no quarrel, you and I." Her eyes rolling up to consider, she tilted her head. "Although you did hide this girl from me for a significant amount of time and tried to deceive me too." She gave me an expectant look. "Why?"

I shrugged. I didn't need to lie. "I was concerned that my life clock was slowing. I needed to extract the magic of her heart to fix it."

"Ah, I see." The Queen sat back, her fingers steepled before her. "Not only that of course. You must have also wanted to overthrow me with the power of the *coeur*?"

A nerve ticked in my cheek, but this was no secret either. "It crossed my mind."

The Queen laughed again. "That's what I like about you, Rabb. You can be quite honest when you want to be." She leaned forward, her eyes gleaming. "Would you...like me to fix your life clock?"

I nearly winced at her offer, but I wasn't innocent in the ways of the world either. "In exchange for what?"

"Well, naturally, if you ask something of me, I must ask something of you."

I kept my voice steady. "Name it."

A corner of the Queen's lips lifted. "Make a bargain with

me then," she proposed. "Do not interfere with the girl to-night. Let me find her a place in Wünder. And I shall happily help restore your life clock. Not only that," she went on as if a fresh thought struck her, "if you keep to your word, I shall give you that one other thing you've always desired."

Almost involuntarily, the heart in my chest began to pound once again.

The Queen grinned. "Do this one simple thing for me, Rabb. Be a good boy, and in return, I shall cut off your leash."

I almost sucked in my breath in eager anticipation.

Freedom.

The Queen was offering my freedom in exchange for something I was already going to be doing regardless. My life clock would be restored and I would no longer be required to do the Queen's bidding. For the rest of my immortal existence. It was too tempting not to consider.

I was certain the Queen had an underlying plan, but it wasn't immediately obvious. I couldn't hesitate for too long to think about it. I narrowed my eyes. "And if I break our bargain?"

The Queen clutched at her chest. "Breaking our bargain? My darling, why think of something so inconceivable right from the start?" She sank back in her seat once more. "I think you already know the punishment for displeasing the Queen."

My entire life's service was already dedicated to her. There was only one more punishment left to be rendered. Incidentally, the Queen's most favored punishment to render.

I would lose my head.

"Why?" I attempted to rationalize my defense. "Aren't I

more useful to you as an assassin? As your most talented sorcerer?"

"Why, my dear?" the Queen mused. "But for no other purpose of course other than I would find it exceedingly amusing." Her malevolent laughter was a cackle that echoed all down the halls and out the front doors. I wouldn't have been surprised if it gave the gardeners a fright.

Swallowing hard, I knew I had no choice. I gave her a curt nod.

The Queen's smile quirked once again. "I'm afraid I need more than a nod, Rabb. Say the words."

I met her sharp gaze. "I agree to your terms."

"Excellent," she remarked. "We have a deal then."

I took a steadying breath but as I moved to leave, the Queen clicked her tongue, and I glanced back.

"My darling, our business is not yet concluded."

I blinked. I wasn't even able to guess what she'd meant before I was struck with an invisible blow. My knees buckling, I collapsed to the tiled floor with a groan.

"You did willfully deceive me, Rabb," the Queen said again. "You need to be punished."

Supporting my weight with my hand braced on the floor, I steeled myself in preparation. This wasn't the first time I had received such punishment from the Queen. There was no talking my way out of it and it was best if I let her have her way.

"I need to ensure that everyone in Wünder understands. This is not acceptable behavior." The Queen rose from her seat to peer down at me. "Do you understand what you've done wrong, Rabb?"

Gritting my teeth, I nodded again.

"Look at me, Rabb, darling," the Queen commanded.

I slowly slid my begrudging gaze up to meet hers.

The Queen's smile quirked once again, her lips parting. "Ah, that stubborn, handsome face," she chided in a merry tone, almost offhand. "You look just like your father."

My heart dropped to my stomach with a thud.

I froze. What?

All at once, my mind spun. My father? I wasn't even aware I had family, let alone a father. My earliest memories were only of being a rabbit, alone, hunted, wounded in the forest. Try as I might, I couldn't capture one fragment of anything to do with my having had a family. How could the Queen possibly know anything about it?

The Queen's eyes lit up at the questions behind my eyes. Her grin turned to a slight grimace and she waved to dismiss it. "Never mind. Forget I said anything." With another wave of her hand, a crackling force of lightning streaked in the air, its malevolent force crashing down on my form.

Grunting, I tried to muffle my pained cry, resisting the urge to collapse facedown at the Queen's feet right then. I called upon my own magic to shield me in part as it didn't amuse the Queen if I was too weak to receive her punishment either. I knew it would only end up being worse for me.

One of the guards leaned in slightly to ask, "Would you like us to close the doors, Your Majesty?"

"Not today, I think. I think today I would like the kingdom to hear Rabb's pain," she declared as she raised both her hands toward me again.

I squeezed my eyes shut as the lightning lashings slammed

down on me once again. My vision turned white. I crumpled lower over my knees.

As the Queen continued, I swallowed the groans in my throat until I could no longer hold them in, until my magic defense weakened altogether. And with her next strike, I exploded in a crying, agonized roar.

She was the Queen of Hearts.

My magic was nothing against hers.

I was nothing.

19

Chapter Nineteen - I Chose This

I spent the rest of the day meditating in my chambers to recover. Attempting to resist the Queen's torture sapped my magic once again and the overnight tides were still hours yet away.

The orange sun threw long shadows against the walls as I strode down the castle hallways. It was a struggle to restrain the urge to check on Allie.

At the very least, I was assured she wasn't in any danger. That much I could tell.

I felt no pain, no distress, nothing beyond the understandable measure of her apprehension to be within the daunting walls of the Queen who might at any moment try to eat her heart and kill her.

Hesitating by the turn in the hallway which as I'd managed

to coerce out of Two led to her room, I shook my head briskly to clear it before whirling back around.

Allie didn't want to see me anyway.

Turning down one of the corridors which looked out to the castle gardens, I stopped to glance out the arched window. A croquet game was underway on the rolling green lawns.

As the Duchess had mentioned, the Queen often put the games on for her amusement. She enjoyed watching her subjects falter and stumble with faulty mallets and moving targets. It seemed the day's choice of mallet was some flamingos held upside-down whilst balled-up hedgehogs rolled across the grass.

Pausing to lean against the windowsill, I observed a little boy from the royal court attempt a shot. Shadowed by an older man in a formal uniform, his hand on the boy's shoulder, the man still smiled when the boy missed widely. Then bending down, the man must have been whispering words of encouragement to the frustrated little boy.

You look just like your father...

The heart in my chest began to pound—erratic, hard.

What the...?

I let out a short grunt and clutched at my chest.

Without warning, the shadows in my chilling visions filled my eyes once again. Just as when I was at the Hatter's merry-go-round, a flash of terrifying shadows and memories of screams plundered through my mind.

The blur of shadowy figures... I blinked twice and I could finally see them. Figures of people. All around me. Fear. Agony. Distress. The Queen's silhouette soaring over everything, as though she owned the violet sky, as she laughed that malevolent laugh.

It was dusk then too.

When my family was killed...

Hopelessness stabbed at my chest, squeezing my heart.

Groaning in frustration, I staggered across the hall, almost missing the doorway to my chambers. I only managed to take two steps in before I collapsed to my knees.

This pain was different from the Queen's lashings, but it was just as intense. The Queen's lashings hurt my body. This hurt my heart with stabbing despair, as though my heart kept exploding into a thousand pieces over and over again.

"Oh god, Rabb! Are you okay?" Allie's voice was panicked as her arm came around my back.

I was in too much pain I didn't even notice her come in. I squeezed my eyes shut. I crumpled over as the stabbing in my chest intensified and I buried my face in my hands. My chest was burning, like it was being torn apart—like *I* was being torn apart.

"Rabb, what's going on?" Allie wanted to know. "Please tell me."

"The shadows, they grow bigger. I think I'm remembering..." I mumbled.

"Remembering what?"

"When I lost my family..." The truth sank in my stomach like a cold frost. "It was her...the Queen. She killed them all. Like animals. They became animals and she hunted them all down. I lost...everyone. That day, it was like my heart was torn out of my chest and broken into a thousand pieces." My voice cracked, every gasp of breath was ice in my lungs.

"Oh, Rabb, I'm so sorry..." Allie's voice was choked, as though the words hurt her too.

Tears stung my eyes but I didn't let them fall. "I almost escaped. I hid in the woods for days. I was the smallest one but she found me. I didn't want to remember. I didn't want to feel anything," I confessed, my jaw clenched. "And the Queen, she made me an offer to take the feelings away. It wasn't going to hurt anymore. She said I was going to be the one to tear out hearts now." The realization sinking in once again as I remembered, I nodded at the floor. "I chose this. I agreed. This is what I wanted. I remember now."

Another wave of anguish and helplessness threatened to bring me to my knees again. I groaned out loud in protest, in indignation.

When Allie sank to put her hand on my shoulder again, I pushed her away. "This is all your fault! You broke me," I accused. "Because of this heart." I clutched at my chest. "I get hurt when you get hurt. Not only that. I can feel what you feel—what I feel. It's been hell. Why can't these feelings just go away? I don't want them. I don't need them! God—how can you people stand them? They're all so confusing!"

"I-I don't know," Allie asserted. "We just do, I guess. Perhaps because you haven't learned to deal with them, they hurt you more." This time, when she put her hand on my back again, I didn't resist. "As a scientist, I think I've never relied on feelings. I've always treasured logic. Maybe that's why I couldn't make myself care about someone else because it just didn't make any sense," she reasoned. "But here, nothing makes sense. And...I'm starting to think that maybe feelings are more useful than I thought. Feelings make us stronger. Feelings help us endure."

My face was too hot. I was way past begging. "Please. Is there anything—I need medicine for this pain."

Allie grimaced. "I'm afraid pains of the heart have no medicines, Rabb."

I shook my head, trying to straighten up but nearly stumbling over. A massive weight of guilt pressed on my chest, the weight of the spirits of everyone I'd hurt as an assassin. "It doesn't matter. You were right. I deserve this. I deserve this for everything I've done. I've killed so many people…"

Allie caught my arm. "No!" she argued, her conviction sharp. "It's not your fault. Your human feelings were torn out of you. You couldn't feel sympathy or compassion. You had no control over what you were doing. You didn't realize what you were doing was wrong."

She stroked my back up and down and somehow, the discomfort in my chest began to dissipate. Her warmth, her closeness washed over me. Her soft words were a balm, soothing my aching soul. "You steal people's hearts and they turn into ghosts, but the truth is you have been the living ghost all this time. I-I understand… I understand now, Rabb—"

A knock on my door made Allie jump.

It was Five. "Miss Allie, there you are. The maids are ready for you."

"Oh, crapshoot," Allie cursed. She frowned before meeting my gaze with a plea in hers. "I have to go get changed for the ball. I'm so sorry."

Taking a deep steadying breath, I took a long moment to compose myself. Dropping my gaze for a moment, I shook my head. Sensing a fresh wave of sympathy and care from Allie, the tension in my body was finally easing, the darkness being displaced by light. I cleared my throat. "There's no need to be. I am fine."

When I met her gaze again, the pure concern and worry in those honey-brown eyes sent a fresh jolt of feelings to my chest, but this time they didn't hurt.

Even as Allie was standing two whole feet away, I felt a tug toward her, the warmth in the space between us undeniably inviting as I held her gaze in the tenuous silence.

The murmured words slipped out of me, "Thank you."

Unbidden, Allie's gaze dropped to my mouth. The heart in my chest started drumming away once again, and for some reason, her forehead creased in curiosity.

I narrowed my eyes, watching the expression in hers change.

It was as if she was...straining to hear something. The gears in her mind were working once again. But after a split second, she blinked in surprise and whirled to leave.

I swallowed hard as she exited my chambers.

For the first time ever, I was curious.

20

Chapter Twenty
- Eligible

It was almost too bright.

The large ballroom at the Queen's castle was haphazardly but lavishly decorated. Floor-to-ceiling windows decked with curtains, red painted over white, so fresh the colors still dripped on the checkered marble floor. Oversized playing cards hanging from the ceiling and ornate chandeliers cast a warm, golden glow on the festivities. The Queen's soldiers, dressed in their vivid tartan uniforms, lined the perimeter of the dance floor like a frame. Diagonal tables were set out on the fringes, along with awkward, slanted chairs that nobody could sit on. Nobody was allowed to sit. Everyone was required to dance.

Musicians dressed in elaborate glittering masks and fascinators played whimsical, offbeat music. The dance floor was

199

alive with a peculiar mix of Wünder citizens and royals twirling and dancing in their eccentric costumes of silk, feathers, sequins, and glitter.

Notably, most of the merry courtiers and nobles were congregated at the front end of the room.

Away from me.

I was nursing my whiskey at a tall table I had conjured up by the sidelines near the grand staircase.

Everyone knew well enough to avoid me. Everyone knew who I was, what I did.

Princes and escorts twirled their lovely dancing partners in the farthest area of the dance floor, wary not to stray too close to my natural charms, or happen to find themselves on the wrong end of my heart-carving skills.

The Queen of Hearts was a vision herself, dressed in her resplendent regalia, sitting on a less elaborate but just as giant throne at the head of the room.

The heart in my chest squeezed. I willed my hands not to shake as I struggled to block the fresh, horrific images of my family's slaughter from my mind.

I knew it was pointless to be enraged all over again. My knowing this changed nothing.

I didn't remember much else about what had happened. I was certain the Queen wouldn't tell me even if I dared ask.

The reason behind the massacre wasn't clear to me yet, but it wasn't unusual to suppose that the Queen's actions were motivated by one single thing. As they almost always were.

Her pointed nose turned up, the Queen watched the extravagance before her with a pleased smile. The sole purpose of everything here was to amuse her, and like the puppets they were, the citizens of Wünder danced and whirled to the lively music, amidst the twinkling glow of fairy sparkles flitting about.

Chez appeared out of thin air and hopped up onto my table.

"Chez." I acknowledged him with a flat tone as I downed my drink.

I checked my pocket watch, trying to ascertain how much time might be seen as appropriate for me to waste here. This ball was the last place I would have ever wanted to be. In the back of my mind, I was already forming an escape plan. I was certain the Queen was planning some sort of trap for Allie once all this ludicrous dancing was over and I needed to be ready for it.

"The Duchess wishes to see all the frivolity," Chez relayed.

Fetching the looking glass from my pocket, I propped it onto the table. I waved my hand and the mirror glimmered into a vanity mirror with a gilded frame. The Duchess's round face peering around it filled the small reflective surface.

"Last year's ball looked better." She sniffed, almost in a disdain that was obviously masking jealousy.

Chez snickered. "My mistress is a bit displeased that she was not extended an invitation to this particular ball."

"Where's Allie?" the Duchess prompted.

As if on cue, several of the courtiers' eyes roved upward. A titter of gasps and murmurs moved through the colorful crowd.

I glanced up in time to see Allie walk out of one of the rooms right above the ballroom itself. She headed toward the grand staircase, and for the first time in my near-immortal life, my jaw dropped.

It was almost as though she was gliding instead of walking.

Allie's ballgown was rich crimson in hue, with delicate lace and vintage beads. The abundant skirt of the dress flowed to the floor, its train dragging on the polished marble floor behind her. The tight bodice around her waist created a dramatic hourglass silhouette. Her wavy hair was swept up in an intricate braid with delicate ringlets cascading down the sides of her face, almost caressing her bare shoulders. The low cut of the neckline showed off her graceful neck, not to mention accentuated her inviting curves.

She was...breathtaking.

Elegant.

Ravishing.

Her eyes glittering at the finery, Allie's gaze was already roving the opulence surrounding us. There was a soft smile on her face as she descended the stairs, fingers running lightly along the railing.

The heart in my chest beat faster, registering her wonder and fascination.

Her gaze met mine right away. Even from halfway across the room, I could tell Allie's breath caught in her throat.

My heart skipped a beat and my grip on my glass tightened.

I snapped my jaw shut. I couldn't walk up to her. I shouldn't.

Her chest heaving, Allie was frozen in her stance as well.

But before Allie could linger any longer, a gentleman dressed in purple velvet and suede approached to take her arm.

Snapping to attention, Allie broke into another smile and nodded as she let him lead her to the dance floor.

I clenched my jaw. Taking a deep breath, I turned my back to the ballroom to lean against the table. I swirled the remnants of my drink in its glass, trying to focus once again on our escape plan.

"Ooh," the Duchess cooed as she struggled to peer around the room. "I think the Queen has selected some very specific kingdoms to attend this evening. These must be all the eligible royals from all the kingdoms across Wünder."

I blinked. Eligible?

Chez scratched his furry chin. "Perhaps the Queen wants Allie to be placed into another kingdom."

"I suppose that makes sense," the Duchess rationalized. "She's of a good age to be wedded."

I glanced over my shoulder just as a prince from another smaller kingdom whisked Allie away. That nerve ticked in my cheek again. This time, I couldn't look away. I wanted to see. I wanted to watch in case I spotted a clue in their interactions that might confirm the Duchess's assertions.

Eligible? The word repeated in my head like a scream, a taunt. I had another urge to flip the table right over.

"Do you think all these men are bespelled to be attracted to Allie?" Chez mused out loud.

I almost scoffed in mocking. She was already the most beautiful thing in the room. I couldn't help a brusque murmur. "She doesn't need it."

"There's a veil over this party."

My gaze snapped back to the cat. "A spell?"

"Some sort of honesty spell," Chez relayed, his nose high in the air as he sniffed.

I huffed again. Such weak spells would not affect sorcerers like *me* but...

The Duchess let out a curious swoon. "Ooh, I suppose the Queen didn't want all these eligible bachelors to lie about their prospects so that Allie could choose fairly."

An undefined aching in my chest warred with the joy I was feeling from Allie. She was laughing at some lame joke from another gallant courtier. Some measure of wanting to rip him to shreds was nagging in the back of my mind. I didn't want that courtier laughing with her, touching her arm, whispering in her ear.

That almost stolen moment Allie and I had at the clock tower before the Queen's invite flooded my senses. The feel of her in my arms, that scent wrapped all around me as I held her. My neck burned at the recollection. I'd wanted to stay like that. I'd wanted...

I frowned as I recalled the Duchess's words from before.

If she falls for you too...

Too...

Was it even possible? Had I fallen for Allie?

How could it be possible for me to have fallen in love at all?

I had no heart of my own. I had been rendered devoid of feelings for centuries.

Was having Allie's beating heart inside my chest changing me? Or could these perhaps be mere echoes of Allie's own feelings? Was *she* starting to feel warmly toward me? And were these her feelings reflected on me?

What makes you think I want to stay here forever?

Deeply frustrated, I shook my head to clear it.

They couldn't be Allie's.

The Queen standing up from her throne caught my eye, as it did everyone else's. I imagined the Queen was about to give a tour, showing off the marvelous hedge mazes behind the castle as she was wont to do, and leave everyone else to their merrymaking.

"Oh! Did you see that lady there with the big, ugly—" The Duchess's disparaging statement cut short as she disappeared from the mirror, leaving only the view of her conservatory of plants behind her, but her voice was floating through, "Hold on, Ham. I'm talking to my Rabb."

"What?" The Duchess's tone turned ominous. "What?" When she asked again, my alerted gaze snapped over to the small mirror. The Duchess's tone was tinged with a dread that instantly filled every kind of suspicion in my mind.

"Duchess?" I prompted.

Chez glanced from me to the mirror, his interest piqued.

The Duchess's round face returned to the mirror, her eyes already marred with concern. "Rabb, I'm afraid I have some news."

I clenched my fists on the table. "What is it?"

"One of my servants overheard the castle staff," the Duchess relayed. "It *is* a trick. We were correct. The Queen is trying to marry off Allie. But more than that. If Allie chooses to give her love freely to any of these men, her heart will unlock and the Queen will be able to claim it."

Rage surged in my chest. What?

The Duchess shook her head. "I told you, Rabb. If her heart fills with love, she is lost."

The trap wasn't after the ball. The ball *was* the trap.

I gritted my teeth as a powerful, hot streak of anger and frustration welled up inside me, nearly overflowing. I almost felt my skin sizzle with the overwhelming burn, which if I didn't keep in check, might actually set the entire ball on fire.

No. I had to make sure none of these unworthy oafs left Allie with a good enough impression for her to fall for them.

I stopped short, my bargain with the Queen screaming back to my mind.

I wasn't meant to interfere.

I was supposed to stay away.

I glanced toward the glass doors leading to the gardens through which the Queen and some guests had disappeared.

Before I broke the stem of the delicate glass in my hand in frustration, I set my drink down.

To hell with it.

My eyes pinned solely on Allie, I stalked toward the middle of the dance floor. The ballroom could have been filled with twice as many people. I would only have seen her.

The crowds parted instantly to give me a wide berth. Nobody missed my approach, except Allie.

Belatedly noticing her partner had stopped dancing, Allie paused in mid-whirl. Catching sight of my forbidding form right behind her, her gasp caught in her throat once again. Surprised, she straightened up. "Rabb, what—?"

I cut her off. "Come with me."

Blinking, Allie bit her lip but she merely turned to give her current oaf an apologetic look before turning on her heels to follow me across the room.

Stopping near the edge of the dance floor, I held my hand out to her. "Take my hand."

Her hand was warm when she placed it in mine. Giving her a slight tug closer, I propped my other hand on her lower back just as the strains of music began.

I wasn't meant to interfere.

But, I rationalized, *it was just one dance...*

An eerie orchestral waltz reverberated within the hall from the masked musicians and I took one step to gently lead Allie, gliding to one side in a box step, in time to the lilting rhythm of the three-beat measure.

Forward step, side step, close step, backward step...and then again.

Her honey-brown gaze never left mine as we swept across the floor in a continuous rotation.

The skirt of Allie's gown flowing behind her, she moved gracefully as I led with each step. Her hair fluttered as she swayed from side to side, around me.

All I needed to do was make it look like I already had her favor to intimidate the rest of her prospective suitors. When I shifted my hands on her back, inwardly I reveled in the gratifying sense that Allie wasn't pulling away from my notably possessive hold.

Allie's gaze on me was almost imploring, tentative.

But above all, always curious.

When she gently interlaced her fingers with mine, the length of my arm tingled.

As the enchanting music swelled, I twirled her out and when I pulled her back against me—too close, her warm breath grazed my cheek. Her intoxicating fragrance filled my lungs. Allie's cheeks tinged pink. I couldn't help my gaze dropping to those sweet, red lips.

I started to ache.

To want.

Blinking quickly to clear my head at the dangerous thoughts, I pulled back again. Making sure to keep a good distance from the warmth of her body, we danced until the soft strains of ominous music faded away.

Just one dance.

I dropped her arms unceremoniously and spun to leave. Regret weighed on my chest in an instant. I'd made a bargain that I wouldn't interfere. The Queen would have my head. My mind raged in near helpless frustration. She was never going to be mine anyway. Could I sacrifice Allie to the Queen's evil plot? In exchange for my survival? My freedom?

I climbed up the stairs. I had no desire to stay at the ball any longer. I didn't want to stand and watch Allie meet and dance with more suitable royals seeking to wed her.

In my haste to leave, I must have missed Allie's withdrawal from the ball. She was clattering up the stairs to follow me. Turning in surprise, I paused in mid-stride.

Allie stopped by the upstairs railing. "Rabb, are you okay?" She peered at me, that crease of concern back on her forehead.

Still frustrated, I shook my head. "I'm sorry. I thought I had to interrupt you. I can't explain right now but—"

She waved my explanation away. "Oh, no, please, it was fine," she assured. "You actually saved me from trying to find an excuse to get away." A sheepish smile came to her face. "It was amusing for a start. Everyone was so friendly. But to be honest, this really isn't my kind of...occasion."

Sighing, Allie fiddled with the beads on her skirt. "I don't suppose it's yours either."

I didn't bother to respond as the statement stood for itself. Given our short period of acquaintance, she certainly knew me well enough.

For a few moments, we both simply watched the goings-on of the festivities below us.

She leaned her elbows against the balcony. "I have to say this is significantly more enjoyable than the last banquet I attended."

I cringed. She was referring to the Veridia wedding where I had massacred everyone.

I, the monster.

Tamping down the urge to tear my own hair out, I resolved to accept the inevitable. Or if I couldn't accept it, perhaps I could be honorable enough to at least acknowledge it. "Have you thought about what the Queen said? Did any of the other kingdoms seem appealing to you? Somewhere you might find your place?"

She pursed her lips in thought. "I don't know. I sort of got the feeling that the Queen seemed intent on marrying me off, but really, I just need somewhere to live. I suppose that caterpillar was right. I would get used to life here eventually." She shrugged. "Honestly, I'd be happy in any kingdom that gave me a workshop, a small space to build my machines and experiments."

The heart in my chest skipped a beat.

Because I could give her that. My clock tower already

had that space for a workshop for her. Not a kingdom, but...something.

"You know," Allie went on to venture. "Somewhere quiet, somewhere away from everything..." She added offhandedly, "I don't even care if it's a bit cramped, as long as it's a nice, cozy place with a great view, perhaps somewhere high up..."

A bit puzzled, I met her gaze.

Wait—was she actually describing my clock tower?

I furrowed my eyebrows. "What are you saying? Are you saying you want to—" I stopped. "Allie, are you saying you want to stay with me?"

At the incredulity in my tone, her face fell. "I know I'm a nuisance, a bother—"

"No." I stopped her right away since it wasn't mocking in my tone, just perhaps a sheer sense of relief or perhaps disbelief.

My eyes caught the faint red glow of magic carpeted above the ballroom.

The truth spell.

Allie may have been immune to my spells but perhaps she wasn't immune to this. I replayed what she'd said in my head. I wanted her to say it again so I could be sure.

Her gaze dropped, she fidgeted on her feet. "Earlier, in your chambers, I thought...I could feel you."

I blinked, stunned.

All this time, because I carried her heart, I had been feeling her feelings. But perhaps it had only seemed one-sided because I'd never had real feelings for her to feel in return before.

"Oh god, maybe I was merely projecting my own want

onto you. Maybe I just imagined it." She averted her gaze, an almost embarrassed flush on her cheeks. "But I thought I could see myself...in the way that you were seeing me. And—it was...lovely."

I couldn't help the blooming warmth of release spreading inside me at her words, at the soft smile on her face.

The heart in my chest started to beat faster. I shook my head, murmuring, "You didn't imagine it." Perhaps Allie had no idea how beautiful she was. Her spirit. Her curiosity. That stubborn-ass courage. "You are more than lovely." I couldn't help the husky rasp in my tone. "And the only thing that's wrong with you is...you said you weren't mine."

Allie visibly swallowed, almost as though she was concealing her elation. Her forehead creased in a slight uncertainty, she gazed up at me in wonder. "You want me...?"

The heart in my chest pounded harder as the truth sank in. "And...you..." I almost couldn't believe I was about to speak the words. "You want me..."

She let out a nervous laugh, leaning back against the railing, unintentionally exposing more of that beautiful bare neck. Her voice shook to remark, "Feelings, huh?"

This woman... I had to resist the most powerful, savage impulse to swoop down and taste that neck, to claim her right then and there... Or perhaps throttle her right then and there. *This* woman...

Scrunching her nose up at me, Allie lifted her hand. "You've got a bit of confetti in your hair—"

I caught her hand fast, her gasp was nearly inaudible as she met my gaze again.

Her honey-brown eyes glittered.

I had quite literally never felt this way before.

My stomach was in knots. It was as though I couldn't breathe. My chest felt tight. I wanted to keep staring into her eyes. I wanted to bask in her smiles, touch her face, take her in my arms, and never, ever let go.

I craved her.

Swallowing hard, I turned her hand toward my face, unable to help the urge to press my lips against her palm. I felt her warmth. I brushed a soft kiss along the sensitive skin of her inner wrist.

Her breath hitching, her mouth dropped open—but not in protest. She wasn't pushing me away. Instead, she pressed her free hand against my chest. There was a quirk in her smile. "My heart is beating so fast..."

I bent my head, my face hovering close to hers, my voice dropping to a low husk as her closeness already mesmerized me. "What are we doing?"

Leaning against me, she tilted her head up, her eyelids half-closing. "Something mad."

21

Chapter Twenty-One - The Truth

"We shouldn't do this." My whisper was hoarse with need even as I walked her backward into her darkened room.

"I know," she said even as she reached for me.

My mouth met hers in the dark, my eager tongue slipping between her welcoming lips, seeking hers, melding with her heat. "You taste so sweet," I almost growled. My fingers tangled in her thick mass of fragrant hair as I devoured her again, claiming her.

Her fingers clutched at my chest. She moaned in my mouth.

My groan rumbled in my chest at her soft sound of surrender. "I want this so badly," I murmured against her lips. "I want you." I broke off to gaze into her sparkling eyes. I swallowed hard, my face contorting in remorse. "I know

I shouldn't. But—" I caressed her flushed cheek, my thumb stroking her already swollen bottom lip.

She nipped my thumb between her lips. Her chest heaved, her breathing labored. Her scent filled my senses. She overflowed with desire. She couldn't hold it back anymore either. Whether it was caused by the veil of magic or her own want, as soon as the door shut behind us, I knew there was only going to be one outcome tonight.

I was going to have her.

And once I unlocked her heart, the Queen would finally be able to take it.

With one last-ditch attempt to restrain myself, I cleared my throat. "Allie, if you give yourself to me... It's too dangerous. We can't let the Queen have your heart."

Allie shook her head. "I won't let her. My heart is yours. Only yours."

There was that reckless, stubborn courage again. How could I possibly fight it?

My chest ached in helplessness. I couldn't help trailing my finger down her soft cheek, that elegant neck. I traced the bare skin on the curve of her neck, the thin, jeweled strap of her gown. Before I could stop myself, I slipped my thumb beneath the beaded string to slide it off her shoulder.

With another groan, I bent my head to taste her there, running my tongue over her smooth skin as I dragged open-mouthed kisses across her shoulder, her neck.

She moaned again and instead of pushing away, she grabbed my head as if encouraging me to keep going.

I lifted my head, glassy eyes meeting hers. "I-I can't stop, Allie. I need you."

"I know," she whispered.

"We shouldn't."

She shook her head, meeting my gaze evenly. "I don't care."

I gazed into her lustrous honey-brown gaze in absolute reverence.

Once again, I was awestruck by her simple beauty. Indignation tore at my chest in absolute understanding that I likely didn't deserve this pleasure at all. I was the last man on Wünder who could possibly be worthy of her. But I needed to be worthy of her. I needed to fulfill her every need, satisfy her every desire.

This was where I belonged. Under her skin. In her heart. The only way I could go on. There was no more living without her by my side. She was my life.

I cast a spell and a glittery yellow fog covered us.

"What's...what is that?" Allie asked, breathless, looking around us.

I couldn't help the surge of relief in my chest. With her heart open to me, she could finally see my spells. "My gift." A corner of my mouth turned up, almost mischievously. "Allie...can you feel me?"

Her eyes widening, Allie's mouth fell open as her pleasure intensified. "Rabb, oh my god—," she rasped. "It's so—it feels so—"

Her response stoked my fire further. I growled and when I backed her up again, the back of her knees hit the bed. "Allie..." I implored one last time. "Tell me you want this."

She swallowed hard, her eyes glazed, consumed with passion. Her husky response was my undoing. "I want you."

It was done.

Allie's fate was sealed.

So was mine.

***

I couldn't have been asleep for more than a minute.

I'd really tried not to fall asleep.

But ensconced in Allie's warmth, that soothing, calming scent wrapped around me... I was defenseless.

When I woke with a startle, the space beside me in bed was already cold.

Alarmed, I shot off the bed to throw my clothes back on.

No. Dear god, please no.

Out the window, the sky was only starting to turn light. The merrymaking and music from the Queen's ball downstairs had already hushed. The castle was quiet.

It was too much to hope that Allie had simply gotten up for a drink of water or to use the washroom.

Before, while she slept, I'd held her tight in my arms. I'd sworn to myself I was never going to let her go ever again.

The escape plan I had been hatching all night had fully developed in my mind.

I was going to take Allie. We would escape the Queen's castle and run away.

We needed someplace to go, someplace I could possibly hide her.

The first option was for us to seek refuge on the River of Tears. Without magic, Allie might find some measure of safety from the Queen's wrath.

The second, less desirable option was that I would return

her heart and then persuade the Hatter to use the tree hollow to send Allie home.

No matter what the Hatter asked for in exchange, whatever it took, I was going to protect Allie.

My chest ached as I set to cursing and blaming myself. This was all my fault. I should have cast some sort of spell to stay awake. Or a spell to keep Allie in the room. A spell to keep her bound to my side. *Something.*

Bolting out the door, I peered down the railing to the ballroom. Empty. Even in the dim light, not even a trace of the previous evening's gathering had been left.

Using stealth and magic, I slipped downstairs, past all the Queen's guards, and hurried toward the throne room. But when I pushed open the double doors, the massive chamber was empty as well.

Allie...

There was no other explanation.

The Queen had taken Allie.

But then stopping short, I clutched at my chest.

Allie's heart.

I still had it.

It beat steadily beneath my palm, then harder.

I squeezed my eyes shut for a moment to concentrate.

Rabb...

A faint white glow glimmered from my chest.

Heaving in relief, in understanding, I strode down the hallways with fresh urgency.

Allie was calling her heart.

She was calling for me.

I wasn't under any illusions that this wasn't a trap, but if Allie was in danger, I had to save her.

Stepping carefully down the stone steps into the crypts underneath the castle, the dank and musty air chilled my skin.

I felt it already.

Extraordinary power was seeping from the room at the far end of the hall. Rushing straight on, I plowed through the doors.

When my eyes adjusted to the darkness of the crypt, it wasn't a crypt at all.

The grand and imposing courtroom had towering ceilings and candle-lit chandeliers which cast a warm glow over the space. Empty wooden benches lining the chambers complemented the sparse, austere decor. At the front, a raised platform held a throne-like, richly upholstered chair before a table whereupon a gavel rested. It was where the Queen would usually sit for official court proceedings.

Dressed in vivid, resplendent red once again, however, the Queen had elected to stand beside the podium where a large cage contained Allie. Allie was back in her own clothes.

I couldn't help the relief flooding my chest. Seeing Allie alive, seeing that decidedly annoyed crease of indignation across her forehead as she gripped the black, metal bars.

Not startled at all about my arrival, the Queen's smile widened as she met my gaze. One of her eyebrows rose in reprimand, her drawl tinged with amusement. "You're late. I expected you to find us much earlier."

22

Chapter Twenty-Two - Heartfire

A rise of anger surging in my chest, I waved my arm to fire a spell, almost on instinct.

The Queen easily deflected my spell. She cackled. "Ah, Rabb. Always so aggressive."

I shot her a glare that could cut as I moved to stand in a defensive pose, ready to fire again. "Let Allie go."

"Keep firing and see what happens to your precious Allie," the Queen proposed with a catch in her tone. "Honestly, Rabb, as you can plainly see, I have not harmed a single hair on her head."

Still wary, I glanced over at Allie. My chest already ached with remorse. This was all my fault. "Allie, are you...?"

Allie waved quickly. "I'm fine, Rabb. She doesn't want

me. She wants—" Her lips pressed shut as the Queen cast another spell.

The Queen grinned. "Now, now, let's not ruin the suspense."

Allie clutched at her mouth in protest but it seemed the Queen was not going to let her speak.

My jaw clenched again. I slid my molten gaze over to meet the Queen's still-amused eyes. "You," I growled low. "You already killed my family and took everything away from me. Tell me why I shouldn't break your neck right now."

Smirking, the Queen shifted on her feet to square off with me. "What a happy coincidence that your memories have returned," she remarked. "But perhaps I shouldn't have been so careless with that spell."

My mouth twitched. "What spell?"

Her expression took on a hazy wistfulness. "When I remembered your father, what I said acted like a spell to unblock your memories."

I stepped back to give her a wide berth as she moved across the room. "Who are you? Why did you kill my family? What do you have to do with my father?"

The Queen contained her chortle in her throat. "Your father? Your illustrious father didn't realize I was the only one who could make him happy. For god's sake, I was the only one with any capacity for amusement at court. And to leave me for that boring woman," she ranted on. "I mean, one might've thought he should have at least tried to fail up."

I blinked. "Boring woman?"

"Your mother, you Tweedle Dumb," the Queen rasped in exasperation.

Another ache stung my chest. *My mother...* Faint memories

of crooning lullabies and warm embraces threatened to constrict my breathing. *My mother...*

"Everyone thought they were so happy. They thought they had the right to be so happy when I was so miserable." Her face crumpled up in disdain before the glint in her eyes turned sly once again. "It really was quite amusing to watch them die together."

It couldn't be. My heart pounded in my chest. *How...* "How does nobody else know this?" I demanded. "How has nobody told me what happened before?"

The Queen smirked. "Perhaps you can already tell I was always quite skilled with fixing memories. Once I had gotten rid of the entire royal family, I made everyone on Wünder forget all about them. All about *you*." She pointed a sharp-nailed finger straight at me before her grin widened. "And the best revenge of all was being able to toy with his beloved son. I thought cursing you to be a rabbit was particularly brilliant, but I confess I found it more amusing to turn you into a heartless assassin who feels no love." Her eyes glowed. "Only I deserve love. And now everyone on Wünder loves only me."

A bitter taste came up my throat. I felt like I was going to be sick. I shot the Queen a cutting glare. "You are mad."

The Queen burst out laughing so hard, tears formed in her eyes. "Darling, this is Wünder. In case you haven't heard, we're all—"

Without warning, I pounced on the Queen with a roar and she fell back with a squeak.

But she didn't protest when I held her down by her throat on the floor. Instead, she choked out another maniacal laugh.

"Oh, please, yes, indeed, try to kill me. Let's see how well that works out for you."

My eyebrows snapping together, I balled up my fist to cast a spell to drain the Queen's magic, but a glowing shimmer enveloped her form.

I swallowed hard. *No.*

The Queen had some sort of protective spell around her.

Her wild eyes gazed up at me. "You can't hurt me. I own you."

With a groan of frustration, I forcibly pushed away from her, backing up halfway across the room once again.

"You don't even understand why I own you." Her hand clutched at her throat, the Queen moved to get up, her skirts rustling. "As soon as I heard that my heartless assassin was falling in love, I knew I couldn't pass up a chance to possess the most powerful Heartfire ember."

I stood in defense once again, blocking my chest with my hand. "You're not getting Allie's heart."

"Not that one, idiot." The Queen moved to throw back a heavy curtain. It was hiding a shelf lined with two active Heartlamps.

I vaguely recognized the smaller ember as the last one I had procured for the Queen, but the other... The other Heartfire ember was not merely faintly glowing. Nearly twice in size as the first, it spouted a brilliant, mystical fire. A full ring of wispy smoke gave it an ethereal glow as it so very subtly throbbed behind the glass.

Bewildered, my eyes widened. The Queen possessed another *coeur*?

"I have to admit, I was glad you found the girl too," the

Queen went on. "I wasn't sure how to slow the degradation of your Heartfire ember."

I swallowed hard.

What. In. The—?

She cast me an amused smirk. "Why did you think your clock tower was slowing, my dear? I knew I shouldn't have tied your existence to such a finicky old thing."

My heart... My entire body chilled in dread. The Queen had possession of my Heartfire ember. All this time. The only reason the Queen was so powerful was because of my heart. A *coeur*.

Allie's eyes were wide in stunned disbelief.

"I tried everything with your stupid Heartfire ember," the Queen confessed with a shake of her head. "I even tried to wear it, but it fought me like a bloody little devil. But now that it's filled with your love, I own the most powerful Heartfire ember in the world."

Her haughty gaze slid back to meet mine as she stepped closer to Allie's cage. "I confess I didn't think it would be this easy for you to forfeit your life and break our bargain. But I guess this girl is really special. Nothing like a healthy dose of jealousy to close the deal."

Meeting Allie's wide-eyed gaze again, my chest heaved. I gritted my teeth. What could I do? I had to do something.

Her lips still pursed together, Allie was repeatedly jerking her head to one side, quite pointedly. She was trying to tell me something but I couldn't decipher what.

When the Queen waved her arm again, my limbs froze. It was as if an invisible hand gripped me. As though I had been captured by the rainbow beast all over again, its vines constricting tight all over my body.

A low growl of protest was trapped in my throat.

"You did this to yourself, Rabb," the Queen declared. "First, I'll drain all of your magic." I grunted again as she lifted me higher, my feet dangling in mid-air. "Then I'll see about cutting off your head in the gardens in the morning. I expect it would be a rather well-attended spectacle, and I wouldn't deprive my people of another fun party."

I couldn't move anything. I felt woozy as my magic siphoned away as the Queen sucked out my soul. My throat was closing up, eyelids threatening to droop. I winced, trying to keep conscious as a noisy clatter drew my attention over the Queen's shoulder.

Allie was thrashing in her cage, kicking at and shaking the bars to no avail. I almost thought she was going to tear her hair out in frustration.

The Queen noticed my glance of concern. She let out a laugh. "Don't worry about her. I'll kill her first so you can watch."

Fresh, molten rage surged in my chest. No. I couldn't let the Queen hurt Allie. The heart in my chest was hammering away in alarm and dread once again.

Tilting her head to one side, the Queen mused, "Would you like me to remove your feelings again? So you don't feel the pain when she dies? You were so desperate last time. Poor little bunny." She tsked. "But I promise you, you will truly be set free. In that regard, it is not I who traps you, Rabb. You are enslaved by that heart."

BOOM!

An intense and blinding flash of light flooded the court-room. My ears rang as I blinked past the spots in my eyes. I glimpsed the flutter of Allie's lab coat as she bolted out of her broken cage.

The Queen's scream was choked as Allie grabbed her around the neck by the crook of one arm, pinned her arms with the other, and squeezed. The Queen screeched, "Off with her head! Off with her head!"

I fell free from up against the wall and crumpled to the floor.

Weak. Drained.

The Queen managed to free one hand and a wave of a quick spell threw Allie off of her.

Allie slid across the floor with a yelp. She was winded. I instantly felt her disorientation.

"You little witch!" the Queen rasped, raising her arms to point at Allie's sagged form as she marched closer. "I'll kill you right now and you can go join your ghost friends in the underworld."

My eyes widened in alarm. "NO!" I grunted through the pain and forced my body to come upright.

I had always thought that humans were made weak by feelings. Feelings hindered actions. But the truth was, ever since I'd had Allie's heart, my magic had been stronger than ever.

With a feral cry, I leaped forward to throw myself in front of Allie, taking the brunt of the Queen's spell. And with the last remnants of my magic, I shot a powerful gust of air to blast the Queen away, sending her tumbling back to blow right through the courtroom chamber doors.

I crashed to the floor and Allie's eyes widened in horror.

"Rabb, no!" For a split second, she touched her mouth, realizing the Queen's spell on her had broken. She sank to the floor with me. "No, crap—" She tried to help me back up. "Rabb, no, dammit—get up."

I stifled a cough. "Allie, I'm so sorry. You have to run. Try to find your way to the river."

She brushed my hair back from my face. "You're such an idiot. Why do you keep jumping in to save me? You said you only wanted to live."

I was spent. My essence was slipping away to join the ghosts, but all I felt was relief. I shook my head. I tried to lift my hand to touch her cheek. "I wanted you. I've only ever wanted you." I managed a weak smile. "Thank you for fixing me."

Allie's jaw clenched. Her gaze dropped in deep thought. The gears in her mind were spinning again.

I frowned at her immobile form. I wanted to yell some more, but my limbs were starting to feel numb. What the hell was she still doing here? I told her to run. Run before it was too late. Run before the Queen—

"You two are starting to annoy me."

Oh. Too late.

Menace in her snarl, the Queen shook off the torn fringes from her gown as she marched back through the broken courtroom doors. "I really liked this dress."

I tried to remain lucid. *Allie, run...* But instead of running away, Allie crouched over to cover my form. She wanted to protect me from the Queen's wrath. She was going to stay with me.

The sudden ache in my chest was accompanied by a warm

surge of power and a shimmery white fog enveloped the two of us.

Allie sat up in surprise. "Rabb, what's...?"

The stinging in my chest grew to a burning fullness—but it was warm, soothing, joyful...

A flash of images rushed through my mind. Allie in my arms when I'd saved her from Tulgey Woods. Me, helping Allie with her injuries at the Duchess's house. How warm she'd felt in my arms when I soothed her at my clock tower. How full she'd felt last night, full of love...

Allie's Heartfire ember had awakened with memories of love.

I blinked in awe, in wonder as fresh, renewed magic flowed through my body. I gazed up at those beautiful honey-brown eyes, utterly speechless. When Allie smiled back at me, I thought my chest was going to explode.

The Queen's remark interrupting the moment, a corner of her mouth quirked up with derision. "Oh, so you've finally ignited her Heartfire ember. Took you long enough. But that measly little new ember will never defeat me." She raised her arms to send a barrage of lashings our way.

Whirling around to cover Allie with my body, I conjured a deflective barrier to protect us.

Still half-squeezing her eyes shut, Allie tugged on my shirt. "I was trying to tell you before. She's only powerful because of *your* heart."

Eyes narrowing, I nodded. My gaze drifted up to the shelf where the Heartlamp held my *coeur*. The Queen had been using and abusing the power of my Heartfire ember all this time.

To end her tyranny, I had to destroy my Heartfire ember.

The Queen caught the focus of my gaze almost too late.

As soon as I raised my hand to summon the Heartlamp, the Queen let out a cry and waved her hand to do the same. A brilliant arc of crackling light shot between our hands as we both tried to retrieve the Heartlamp.

Groaning in the strain, my boots slid back on the floor as I struggled to hold my stance. The Queen's power, amplified by my *coeur*, was too formidable.

Without warning, Allie shot out from behind me. Letting out a savage growl, she leaped onto the Queen's back again. But the Queen was more alert this time. With another wave, Allie's body whipped upward and was clutched in the Queen's invisible hand, to dangle in mid-air as she choked for breath.

All at once, my throat constricted too. My hold on the Heartlamp wavered as I clutched at my neck.

The Queen cackled again. "See what happens when you feel too much?"

Allie's eyes fluttered closed as she started to suffocate in the Queen's python grip.

Allie! My entire being cried out for her. Collapsing to one knee, I swallowed hard. The Queen was going to take someone else I loved. I would be alone again. No...

Feelings make us stronger. Feelings help us endure.

I once had a family who loved me. I wasn't alone. I also had Allie and the strength in her heart was all I needed.

Every nerve in my body strained as I pushed back up. I only had one chance left but I was going to have to use all of my magic for this to work. With an agonized cry, I let the

Heartlamp go and summoned a massive ball of energy to hurl at the Queen. The sheer force of it threw me backward.

The Queen screeched in alarm but with both her hands occupied, she couldn't protect herself from my spell. Tumbling backward, her skirts in her face, the Queen's grip on both Allie and the Heartlamp faltered.

Allie fell to the floor, coughing to regain her breath.

The Heartlamp sailed down and crashed as the brittle glass pieces snapped and splintered across the floor on impact, ringing cracks reverberating in the air. A sharp gust of wind blew through the courtroom chambers, accompanying the tinkling shatter.

The brilliance of the exposed, burning *coeur* on the floor a few feet away filled Allie's wide eyes. She scrambled closer.

"No!" The Queen's eyes widened in alarm and from across the room, she threw a spell to keep the Heartfire ember from Allie's grasp, but the spell merely bounced off.

My burning heart blazed wild, fierce, but Allie showed no hesitation as she picked it up.

"You little—" The Queen stalked toward Allie, red eyes filling with a terrifying menace.

Allie jerked in alarm at her approach. Her eyes darted around for two seconds as if at odds what to do. She couldn't toss the ember over to me. If she dallied any longer, the Queen would regain control of my heart.

Allie clenched her jaw in determination before slamming the burning heart inside her chest. She cried out a gasp at the force.

The Queen of Hearts's source of power was gone.

"No...no..." The Queen stepped back. Shaking all over, she

stumbled over her long skirt and collapsed against the steps leading up to the raised podium. "It can't be. It can't be. You shouldn't be able to." Her eyes widened but she could only watch as Allie's hunched form glowed blindingly bright.

Chains of light streaked through the air as crackling electricity filled the courtroom. With a massive shockwave of energy, a burst of magic surged from the *coeur* and whipped across the room like a gale-force wind.

The shockwave of power shunting through me, I almost tumbled over where I lay.

Allie straightened up, her figure still glowing. Her eyes mere bright slits, she approached the Queen of Hearts who was writhing on the floor from some unseen torture. She glared down at the Queen. "You are so not amusing."

The Queen screamed in terror as her magical essence drained, sucked away by the Heartfire ember in Allie. Her figure seemed to blur and fade, her screams fainter, bit by bit, until no one could hear her cries any longer, and the slumped body on the floor disintegrated into nothingness.

The brilliant glow around Allie's figure ebbed away. She turned to me, breaking into a run to drop to my side. "Rabb, are you okay?" When she met my gaze, the light in those honey-brown eyes was back.

With Allie's heart, I felt an overwhelming sense of relief and love. I touched her cheek. "My hero."

That made Allie laugh.

Trying to sit up, I groaned at the strain. My feelings were fine, but my physical injuries still hurt like hell. The magic of Allie's Heartfire ember was sapped. Blinking slowly, I resisted the need to pass out. "How the hell did you get out of your cage?" I wanted to know. "Was that magic?"

"No." Supporting my back, a grin laced her lips as she spoke, "That was science." She gestured to her pockets. "A bit of alkali, sulfur, magnesium, and voila!" she declared with a wink.

I half-scoffed out a relieved chuckle and moved to stand. "We should probably—"

"Wait." Allie put her hand up and before I could say anything, she grabbed my face for a kiss.

Energizing magic and raw, potent want shot through my body. With her healing kiss, Allie's Heartfire ember transferred a bit of magic into mine. But she broke off after only a moment. "Give it a sec."

Feeling interrupted yet again, I grabbed the nape of her neck to tug her closer once more, my growl low with molten desire. "Give me back that damn mouth."

Allie giggled but obliged as I slanted my lips against hers, kissing her hard, tasting that perfect sweetness, having my fill.

Making up for all the times I'd wanted so badly to kiss her but didn't. Relieving that dreadful fear of having almost just lost her. Fearing I might never get enough of her.

Or...no, I didn't fear that at all.

Pleasurably heady, I only pulled away to breathe.

Dropping her gaze, Allie's cheeks were flushed as she touched her swollen lips.

A warmth spread in my chest as I sensed Allie's contentment and satisfaction. It was all I could do not to lean in and kiss her again. But I didn't want to tire her out—so soon.

There would be more time for that later if I had anything to do with it.

23

Chapter Twenty-Three - Home

Supporting my arm, Allie helped me walk out of the underground crypts to lead me out of the castle. As Allie swung open the double doors, I winced at the bright, glaring light of day.

She took a deep breath as if she were summarizing the events of the day. "So that Queen was some crazy, vengeful ex-lover who killed your father. And your father was the King of Hearts. The true King of Wünder." She cast me a sideways look. "Do you realize what this means, Rabb?"

What this means...

I swallowed hard as a new heavy realization settled within me. I could barely wrap my mind around it. "It means..." I trailed off at the strange lump in my throat.

I was the rightful ruler of Wünder.

A shudder went through me as a subtle pulse shot across the blue sky, to the farthest reaches of the forest and mountains visible from the castle.

"What the hell was that?" Allie's jaw had dropped.

Just as puzzled, I shook my head.

For a moment, the entire castle around us was silent.

With a pop, Chez's fuzzy purple-coated form appeared on top of one of the topiaries flanking the front steps. "So, it's 'Your Highness', isn't it?" He licked a paw. "I knew I sensed something about you."

What? I blinked.

The veil of magic all across the land must have lifted as the wretched Queen of Hearts's memory spell was erased from the minds of all the citizens of Wünder.

With another sharp grunt, I clutched at my core as a fresh slow burn spread throughout my insides.

"Rabb...?" Allie's prompt was already worried but she let her arms drop from me.

I closed my eyes for a moment at the sting but I already knew the fully restored Heartfire ember was healing me from the inside out. I gasped as my injuries and clothes were instantly mended and immaculate.

Then straightening up, I took another deep breath.

Allie breathed, "Oh dear..." Her gaze was distracted over my shoulder.

Lifting my head, I stunned myself as well.

Several of the royal guards and pages from inside the castle had come outside. Their faces were marred with confusion as though having woken from a long sleep.

At the sight of me, one of the pages fell to one knee and bent his head. "Your Highness."

Stepping back, I winced, my chest constricting.

Before the rest of the soldiers could follow suit, I put my hand up. "No. Please," I cut in with a frown. It didn't feel right.

Chez's ghostly head swirled beside mine, his eyes big and yellow. "What's wrong, Rabb? That is who you are."

Remorse filling my chest, I shook my head. "I have a lot to answer for," I admitted. "I've hurt so many of my people."

Chez turned upside-down in thin air with a suggestion. "The Duchess might have a way to help you restore the people's stolen hearts, and the Hatter might be able to help you make peace with the ghosts."

I was still uneasy, but at least if what Chez said was true, there was still hope for me. I gave him a slow nod. "Until I do, I don't think I deserve this."

Allie's smirk was amused. "Look at you, all considerate and...feeling-y."

Powerless against her teasing, I crossed the courtyard in two strides to pull her into my arms. That familiar, comforting softness, that intoxicating scent enveloped my entire being.

Tilting my head down, I peered into her face. "Hi."

Allie's laughter was sweet. She brushed my hair back from my forehead. "Hi." She paused, a mischievous twinkle in her eyes. "We haven't officially met, Your Highness."

I made a face at that and gave her a rueful look. "Well," I pointed out, "we know who *I* am now. But with the wretched

Queen gone, we won't have a way to help you recover your memories."

"I like my memories fine the way they are right now." She gazed up at my face for a moment, her eyes shining. "Besides, I heard what the Queen said," she added with an eager nod. "It's just a spell. It worked for your memories. All I need is the right phrase, the right spell, to unlock mine. Perhaps if I think about it hard enough, I bet I can figure it out."

I sensed no remorse, no disappointment in her self-assured tone. My smile widened in relief, in pride. "If anyone can, I'm sure it's you."

Her vindicated, appreciative smile sent shivers straight through to my core. *This woman...* Leaning my forehead against hers, I dropped a glance down to whisper, "You have my heart."

Her smile widening, Allie pressed her hand against my chest. "And you have mine."

I swallowed hard again, an uneasy hollow in my chest at what I wanted to say next. I didn't want to ask it. I didn't want to even think of it. But I knew it was inevitable. Cradling her face with one hand, I played with the tendrils of her silky hair. "What about going home to your world?"

One corner of her smile quirked up in the most adorable, mischievous smirk. "I'm a genius. I'm sure I'll find a way. Or maybe Your Royal Highness could command the Hatter to recreate that portal doorway if I ever felt like visiting the other world. Either way, we've got plenty of time for that. I think I'd like to stay and explore yours a little bit more."

I pulled her even closer, reveling in her warmth, basking in her smile. The joyous emotions from her Heartfire ember and mine were almost too overwhelming, I worried I was going to burst. "Maybe I'll order the Hatter to destroy that door, so you'll be stuck here with me forever," I teased—half-teased?

Her jaw dropped. "You wouldn't."

"What, you think you can do better than the most powerful sorcerer in Wünder?" I gestured to myself with confidence before stopping to amend. "I'm sorry. Most powerful sorcerer *and* ruler of Wünder?"

Allie shot me an incredulous look. But she merely bit her lip to tamp down an amused chuckle. "You're still ridiculous."

I flashed an airy, self-assured grin.

This was going to be interesting.

* * *

The End

If you enjoyed Rabb's story, you'll love Allie's story coming up next in this series!

Subscribe to S. R. Breaker's mailing list to be the first to hear about new books.

S. R. BREAKER is a USA Today Bestselling Author of non-stop action adventure, offbeat YA/NA fantasy romance books. She lives in New Zealand with her husband and two kids.

Suburban mum by day and author by night, she loves to live vicariously through her characters. They don't have to vacuum all day long and are almost always guaranteed to survive any fantastical or thrilling incidents, no matter how treacherous she writes them.

Subscribe to her mailing list now for bookish news and get a FREE e-book!

https://subscribe.breakerworlds.com/fantasy

Feel like more thrilling, slow-burn, closed-door fantasy romance by S. R. Breaker? With dragons?

Read on for a sneak peek...

Sneak Peek: Curse of the Dragon Heir

A headstrong Fae mage accidentally sets a mysterious evil demon free but he may be the key to unlocking her powers...

"Are you mated yet?" His voice was gruff but deeply rich.

Soleia shot him a glare. "That's none of your business."

The three warrior females exchanged looks.

Oh, great, Soleia thought in derision. Now they were probably going to start rumors about her and the demon. Just what she needed right now. "Thank you for your help." She dismissed the females with a wave before hanging up her cloak and turning back to fix her hair.

His scrutiny was unnerving her and also making her stomach do somersaults.

Stupid stomach. What the hell was wrong with her anyway? He was a cursed, dangerous demon that would destroy them all with one swish of his claws if given half the chance.

She cleared her throat, hurrying to finish grooming so she could exit the cramped indoor space, feeling a bit more cramped than before.

"Let me free."

Her eyebrows rose in incredulity at his words. "So you can kill me and everyone I know?"

He visibly swallowed hard. "I won't."

Soleia gave him a dull look. "Right."

His forehead creased in aggravation. "You don't even know who I am! How do you know it's justified to hold me against my will? How do you know you're not in the wrong here?"

"Look, the only wrong thing I did today was take too long at that dumb wraith forest. I should have ridden faster, fought harder. I should have just left some of the smaller wraiths alone. If I could have just put them to sleep, I could've—" She stopped short, blowing out a frustrated breath.

His eyes narrowed. "I thought you handled yourself quite well."

She gave him a deadpan look. "I know exactly what you're doing. You're trying to ply me with compliments so that I'll feel sorry for you or something and maybe release you from Oma's binding spell. But I'm not that dumb, Curse Boy."

He blinked like he didn't expect her to figure that out and he merely huffed in displeasure and looked away.

Soleia smirked. She was quite enjoying having so much power over him. "What kind of a dumb demon gets trapped on a tree anyway? And then to finally get free of the tree, only to get trapped by a necklace! Is this only the second curse that's been put on you? Or have there been more?"

That set him off.

He growled again, grabbing her by the shoulders and pinning her back against the wall.

She almost rolled her eyes at his futile intimidation efforts. Did he forget one word from her would send him doubling over? She met his gaze, undaunted. "You didn't scare me before. You definitely don't now."

He roared, leaning close to her face. He was clearly displeased, infuriated. "Mark my words," he rasped. "This spell *will* break. And when that time comes, I guarantee you, you *will* be scared. And then you will die."

"Right, whatever. But until then, Curse Boy, your life belongs to me." Soleia gave him a shove to push away but he pressed harder.

He was focused on her mouth. "Dathon," he growled. "My name is Dathon."

He spoke near her face. His freshly showered scent was almost hypnotizing, overwhelming. Her chest heaved against his in her struggle to breathe and he must have noted her heart pounding. His incensed gaze seared into her.

Soleia blinked her senses back into focus and threw up her hands. "Fine!" And at her concession, he let her shrug him off. "Whatever."

* * *

Enjoyed the preview?

Curse of the Dragon Heir is available to purchase at your favorite bookstore!

Reign of the Dragon Heir: Book 2 of "The Dragons of Arcadia" series is out now!

"She must marry to save all the realms. He must marry her to uncover an evil plot. Will their fake match find truth before the world ends in oblivion?"

Feel like more STEM heroes, multiverses, and fast-paced action adventure?

Jump into a portal fantasy sci-fi adventure across the multiverse with S. Breaker's completed series **Selfless**.

"They're after you. But which you...?"

Mistaken for her imperiled, notorious genius alternate self, Laney's accidental trip to a parallel world could very quickly turn very deadly.

Read on for a sneak peek...

Sneak Peek: The Selfless Series

They're after you. But which you…? Mistaken identities. Parallel worlds. Government conspiracies. Out of time. Save the multiverse. Save yourself. Don't get erased. Ready?

"Did we lose them yet?" Laney rubbed her hands over her arms in the freezing cold.

Noah looked intently at the gadget on his arm, tapping a few keys seemingly in mid-air. "I wouldn't count on it."

The rain had abated but it was still dark. It seemed like they had run deeper into the city. She still didn't know where the hell they were.

The whole city was deserted. Old-fashioned cars were stopped in the middle of the streets, some having crashed onto other cars, or onto building facades with faded, cracked brickwork, fallen tarnished bicycles dotted the road, a vaguely iconic-looking red double-decker bus lay on its side at the far end of the street, almost out of view. There was no trace of any other people around, not even animals. Several doors to apartment buildings across the street had been left wide open. It was as though everyone had dropped everything to leave in a hurry.

"What...happened here?" she wanted to know, half-dreading the answer to her question.

"This is the dead city. Ground zero."

"Ground zero. For what?"

He sighed then as if it was no big deal, he relayed, "The global cascade bomb that nearly obliterated all organic life on our world sixty-seven years ago."

"Th-the *what*?" Laney gasped in shock, horrified.

He shot her a slightly annoyed look. "Look, can you keep up? We've already missed the rendezvous window and we're nowhere near where we need to be.

Laney braced her hands on her knees, still trying to catch her breath, and shot him an annoyed look right back. "Hey, we've been running all night. I don't know about the Laney from your world but *this* one is not a triathlon champion."

He didn't respond to her statement. "Come on." He motioned, leading them through a gap in the broken wire fence surrounding a construction site.

"You didn't answer my question earlier," Laney spoke up. "That guy, the one who tried to kill me the other night. He was looking for something. What is it anyway?"

Noah shot her a look, hesitating. "Do you know what spacetime is?"

"Of course," Laney replied dismissively.

He narrowed his eyes at her, dubious.

She blinked again. "I mean," she began. "I know it's like a *science* thing."

"Spacetime is the fabric of the multiverse within which all

our worlds exist," he stated as if he was talking to a child. "Do you know what a wormhole is?"

She pursed her lips.

"What do you learn in school?" he asked in disbelief.

She made another face. "Once again," she said, gesturing to herself from top to bottom. "Normal person. *Not* genius nerd."

Noah rolled his eyes. "Look, the main thing is, there's a device. It makes it possible for a person to move back and forth between two distinct realities."

"Okay."

Noah blinked hard. "No. *Not okay*. What they're ignoring is the probability that this device is going to cause a break in the spacetime continuum, effectively erasing us all from existence. And life as we know it will be over. *Everywhere*."

Laney mused, "I still don't understand what any of this has to do with me."

"Well, obviously, the government bureaucracies in my world really want this device back—badly. And unfortunately, they think *you* have it."

She stifled an incredulous laugh. "Why the heck would they think *that*?"

"Because...you created it, Laney."

* * *

Enjoyed the preview?

The Selfless Series is available to purchase at your favorite bookstore!

www.ingramcontent.com/pod-product-compliance
Lightning Source LLC
Chambersburg PA
CBHW060709190726
48289CB00002B/602